SPACED OUT

INTERPLANETARY VOYAGES OF THE *LINDA RAE*

By KATE THORNTON

To Inna Jane Ray, the real inspiration for the *Linda Rae*.

I couldn't ask for a better sister.

FOREWARD

When I was growing up, a long time ago, we all still had the charming fantasy that space travel – real travel, not just the shuttles and the space station – would somehow be a reality in which we could all share, where jaunts to the Moon and maybe even Mars were commonplace and all sorts of enterprising endeavors would spring up and flourish at the whim of the human race.

This wasn't just the playtime stuff of children that went along with science fiction movies and television adventures, but a sort of accepted future that everyone would experience in their lifetime. In 1960, you could have asked anyone, even my grandma, if we were going to go to Mars or have a base on the Moon, and the answer would have been, "Of course. Now go wash up for dinner."

When we landed on the Moon for real in 1969, it was both the beginning and the end.

Yes, we did a remarkable thing. Yes, we got there. But we didn't go any further. On the 14th of December in 1972, when Gene Cernan last stepped on the lunar surface at Taurus-Littrow, that was it for manned lunar expeditions, and the dream of manned interplanetary flight had to be shelved.

It was just too expensive, too dangerous, politically unpopular and the money – once we had beaten the Russians to the Moon – could be used for other things, other research, and other plans.

So we got the Space Shuttle – with more than our share of excitement, drama, and tragedy – and we got the International Space Station, a miracle of worldwide cooperation.

But manned space travel to the moon and further was left to the dreamers. We may still get there, but it probably won't be for me to see. In the meantime, I'll continue to travel to the stars with a wisecracking pilot named Cookie Sullivan in an old rust-bucket named the *Linda Rae*.

---Kate Thornton

Table of Contents

The Captain's Log

This was the first Cookie Sullivan story and it remains a favorite of mine.

This won't make it into the real captain's log, and you'll be able to guess why, but you know how you always try to cover your ass with something at least the size of your computer screen? Well, this is it.

When we first started commercial shuttle flights to and from places like Mare Tranq on the moon, the shuttles were presumed descended somehow from ocean vessels, don't ask me why, and maritime law was applied in places where the absence of water was second only to the absence of air.

I never did understand how seafaring naval customs got up into the stratosphere and above, but I guess it made things like protocol on board the crafts much easier. I mean, there was a captain and a first officer and even if we were really just shuttle-rats who couldn't get a job anywhere else, we wore the gold braid and carried the traditional powers that ocean-going captains had wielded for thousands of years. We were called pilots, too, something that could cause more confusion than it did back when *The Pirates of Penzance* was first written.

This didn't mean we spent a lot of time making business-class travelers walk the plank, and we didn't sit around hoisting things up yardarms or whatever, either. About the only real traditional duty we had to perform was repelling pirates.

I guess piracy conjures up visions of those same Gilbert and Sullivan swashbucklers in eye patches with cutlasses between their teeth, but on the Mare run, they were sociopaths in light armored spacesuits whose converted speedcraft could overtake a passenger shuttle. They would lock on, blow a hole through the hull, and swarm aboard to rob the passengers and crew. Then they would plunder whatever cargo might be on board and make a hasty exit.

There was one really big problem with this, besides the indignity of being robbed, of course, and that was the gaping hole in the hull. When the pirates disengaged, they sealed their airlock, but did not seal the hole in the plundered craft. The air rapidly leaked out, say in a matter of seconds, causing the whole thing to nearly turn itself inside out with sudden depressurization. Oh, and everyone on board died right away from the same phenomenon. It was messy.

This sort of thing was very bad for business. After three of these attacks, the Corporation decided to arm the shuttles and give the pirates a run for their money. People like me were hired on to captain the shuttles, and the maritime laws were invoked.

I touched the gold braid on my sleeve. Only the top part of it was visible because the uniform irritated me and I rolled the sleeves up as high as they would go. I left the tunic open nearly to the waist, as well. About the only part of the damned thing I could stand was the comfortable pants bloused into really nice boots. I probably would have signed on for a run just for the boots.

"Excuse me, Captain Sullivan," my First Officer was a pain in the ass, a really gorgeous pain in the ass, "but I think you need to fasten your tunic." He stood at attention, eyes straight ahead.

"For what?" I asked. "Are we expecting company?" I just liked to see him sweat when I unbuttoned it. I wore a regulation blouse beneath it, but the fabric was very thin. I had caught him more than once ogling my breasts, which were not only very pretty, but also completely natural. I ran a hand over them. It wasn't nice to torment First Officer N'Doro.

I buttoned up and scanned the new log report N'Doro handed me. He was still at attention. Nearly six feet, the height limit for pilots, he was a recent graduate of the Corporation's shuttle pilot training program. I was a not-so-recent graduate of the school of hard knocks and had received my shuttle pilot's license the old-fashioned way, by running my father's old bucket on early commercial runs and then, after the accident which claimed him and the craft, enlisting in the Corporation's service when they were having a difficult time getting pilots. Later, some whiz kid had the bright idea of a Corporation shuttle pilot school, an academy.

I worked my way up, which wasn't hard the first couple of years. The Corporation would have liked to rid itself of the handful of captains like myself, but there was still a shortage, and now with the piracy thing happening, fewer bright young kids wanted to risk a career as a glorified bus driver on the sudden death run.

"First Officer," I said to N'Doro after looking at the logs, boring as usual, "let's go through the drill in an hour or so." I was referring to the pirate drill the Corporation dreamed up for us. It was a series of defensive maneuvers in the shuttle which ended with a simulated attack and our responses to it. It was the only exciting thing we had out there on the two day run to Mare Tranq, not counting me playing with my blouse.

That particular day we were carrying a bunch of building supplies for a casino, some gourmet foods for a Corporation exec, and twelve passengers, five of whom were party ladies for the pleasure palaces at Mare Tranq. N'Doro and I executed the take off without any problems, put our shuttle, the *Linda Rae*, on auto for the trip, and stayed away from the passengers and the cargo.

The Corporation was pretty strict about the crew staying isolated from whatever was being transported, especially since that incident with the circus troupe and the hospital supplies. The crash site became a popular tourist stop.

N'Doro and I practiced our pirate defense, being careful not to alarm the passengers. Privately, I thought that if anyone ever had a chance of survival in a pirate attack, it would be the ladies we were carrying that trip. Unless the pirates were women, too, not unknown in that sector of space, I mean, look at me.

Once we discharged the cargo and passengers, we would be safe until the next trip. No pirate had ever been stupid enough to attack an empty shuttle, and the return flights were almost always empty, although once in a while you got a couple of folks going back earthside for some reason.

Just when we had worn ourselves out going through the Corporation's little scenario, I heard the warning noise from the console. It was the space-borne equivalent of a curb feeler, letting you know when you were getting too close to something else. Too close was about three earth miles, and the sensor picked up anything larger than a desk - anything large enough to do serious damage in a collision.

This time it wasn't a stray piece of space trash from the satellite frenzy days or a bit of hot meteor. I saw the racing craft on the screen and my stomach lurched. Pirates.

N'Doro kept his cool and began the standard Corporation drill. He flipped up the communicator switch and sent a distress signal, bouncing it by way of Mare Tranq, just in case we were being scrambled by the pirates. Then he checked the outside weapons, a couple of little beam-throwers, and turned off the radio. I dug a couple of sidearms and rifles back out of the storage locker where we had just put them and buckled my old Glock stingray around my waist. I liked the feel of a sidearm, although on a shuttle you could only fire beams of deadly particles, nothing as romantic as lead slugs.

N'Doro buckled his weapon on awkwardly. He had never quite got used to the feel of it, and had never even considered wearing a weapon for most of his sheltered life. The Corporation discouraged it except for piracy drills, but I was used to mine. When I was flying Daddy's old crate, there were plenty of times when a good weapon came in handy.

The pirate craft swooped in quickly. It was small and fast, about half our size and maybe six or seven times our speed. There was no way to outrun it, and by the time anyone got to us from earthside or Mare Tranq, we'd be dust floating in an uncertain orbit.

I thought fast as N'Doro checked the live ammunition in our automatic rifles. Not a whole lot was known about the past attacks because no one had survived. Only the panicky radio signals - just before the blip on the screen blew into a bazillion tiny blips - gave any hint of what had happened.

I hurried out to the passenger compartment and let them know the bad news. The seven business travelers went white and one of them grabbed for a sick bag. The ladies of the evening got very quiet.

"We'll do what we can to defend ourselves," I told them. "Does anyone have anything that might help?"

One of the ladies stood up. She was a big girl, tall and with a lot of weight. She pushed her masses of curly red hair back and said, "Gimme a gun, Captain. The sonsabitches aren't going to take me without a fight!"

The other ladies agreed, but Business Class shrank. One of the Corporation travelers managed to scream out in a high pitched little yowl that *"it was no use and we were all gonna die."* That's what I liked, optimism in the face of danger. And trust me, that little jerk had just named himself First To Be Sacrificed.

I threw Big Red my rifle and motioned for N'Doro to dig out what few remaining weapons we had in the locker. I knew there was a Corporation-issue sidearm in there - the one they had issued me.

"Okay, First Officer," I said as the pirate craft banged into ours. "I guess this is it." I flipped on the little beam weapons on the outside of the *Linda Rae*. They didn't work.

The noise on the side of our hull gave away the pirate location. At least we could be ready for whatever came through the hole. The passengers, except for three armed women, hid back behind the service counter while N'Doro and I flanked the spot where we thought they might be coming through. The armed women took up covered positions like pros.

The force of the explosions knocked us all on our asses, and I struggled to regain control of the Glock. Smoke cleared a bit to reveal a jagged opening in the side of the wall as we were sprayed with beam weapons. The passengers were screaming, the pirates were screaming, the shuttle was groaning and the weapons were making a racket, too. The scream of one of the ladies was cut short by instant death as a beam weapon cut her in two.

Big Red aimed carefully and shot the first pirate who came through the crude door. The beams bounced off the light armor and merely served to attract the pirate's attention. He turned toward her with a large weapon.

I melted the side of his head off with my Glock and he crumpled, an obstacle for the others who tried to swarm through behind him.

Big Red flashed me a grin and dropped to the floor for cover. The next two who came through met similar resistance as Big Red trained her rifle on their unprotected faces. Identification was going to be a problem, I thought, unless these guys had fingerprints or something. The usual biometrics, retinal and facial structure scans, weren't going to have much to go on.

We must have made somebody pretty mad, because a fully armored figure leaped into the shuttle with one of the biggest spray guns I have ever seen.

You know, up until then I had discounted First Officer N'Doro's training as being of the pantywaist fire drill sort. But N'Doro saw an opportunity, and heaved himself through the opening, disappearing into the pirate craft. I couldn't tell if he survived long enough to pick off one or two of the invaders.

I tried to get a good shot at the spray-gun guy, and Big Red was trying to hit him, too, but there was no way to penetrate the armor, and this guy was wearing a full face helmet. Beams pinged off him, and I realized that very soon we would be out of ammunition.

I heard the unmistakable sound of the pirate's airlock closing and sealing. Shit, I thought, if they disconnect now, we're goners.

Spray-gun heard it, too, and whipped around with a yelp. He jumped through the hole in our ship and banged on the airlock with his gun.

I looked around. The deck was covered in blood, and there were at least two pirate bodies down, maybe three. I could see the bodies of two ladies, too, but no sign of Big Red or the business class travelers. I assumed they were all hiding behind the service counter. I hoped they were too scared to make any noise.

Spray-gun turned to me and raised his weapon, then thought better of it. "You!" he said, motioning with it, "Get over by the door!"

I moved slowly to the jagged opening in the hull of my ship. A soft plastic material adhered all around it, sealing it from the vacuum outside. The airlock door to other ship was fitted out with external hardware, something airlock doors never came with. In space, who would come knocking?

Spray-gun rapped on the airlock door. Someone rapped back, but the door didn't budge. Spray-gun aimed his weapon at the door's hardware, then must have remembered that disabling the airlock would trap us all in a bizarre coupling, each ship unable to go anywhere, and when the fuel ran out, we'd be just as dead as if we stepped out into space, only it would be slower and less pleasant.

"Oh, crap," he said disgusted. "You, get over there and get your radio on." He waved the spray-gun around again, so I did as I was told. The radio console was on the bridge, the tiny cubbyhole where N'Doro and I flew the ship. I ducked into it and turned the communications center back on. Crackling static greeted me.

Spray-gun shoved me aside and began fiddling with the controls. "Answer, goddam it!" he shouted.

"Hey, Captain, you there?" N'Doro's voice came through loud and clear.

I grinned. N'Doro had made it. "I'm here," I replied.

"Open the fucking door!" Spray-gun demanded.

"Uh, I don't think so," N'Doro said. "You'd just shoot me and take off. I can't let that happen."

"I'll kill your captain," Spray-gun threatened, "and everyone on board this shit bucket!"

N'Doro seemed to think it over. "No, I don't think so," he said again. "You can kill everyone there if you want to. It doesn't matter to me. I can fly this thing away and just let you all pop like sausages." The prospect seemed to please him.

I got a little nervous and regretted all the teasing I had given N'Doro. Hell, I was only kidding. Couldn't he take a joke?

Spray-gun tried again. "Open the door or I'll kill them all one by one." He looked around. Everyone he could see, except me of course, was already dead. He might have suspected there were others, but he couldn't see them. I weighed the chances of taking him out with my little Glock and the help of whomever was still alive and functional behind the counter before he could spray me with concentrated death. The scales tipped heavily in his favor.

I could hear N'Doro laughing over the radio. "Forget it, pal," he said. "I'm takin' off!" There was an ominous noise as the engines of the speedcraft revved up. N'Doro was testing the controls.

"Wait!" I shouted, "N'Doro! You'll kill us all!"

"Tough break, Captain," he said. "I always wanted my own ship, and this little thing is a beauty."

I just stood there, stunned and enraged. The bastard! Spray-gun wasn't too thrilled with the situation, either. He banged his weapon against the door again and shouted some more obscenities.

"Hey! Wait!" Big Red came out of hiding. Spray-gun wheeled around, weapon drawn. He looked at her, all six feet of voluptuous creamy flesh and gorgeous red hair, and lowered his weapon. Did I mention she had removed her bloodstained jumpsuit?

"Jeezus," he whispered in admiration. I was admiring her too, not so much for her physical attributes as for her nerve.

"Take me with you," she implored the airwaves, her voice reaching N'Doro. "I don't want to go to Tranq, I want to go with you!" She moved toward the door. "Come on, you don't need these losers, but you could use someone like me." N'Doro seemed to hesitate.

Great, I thought. N'Doro and Big Red fly off to happy-ever-after while I get to die with a lunatic pirate, a couple of prostitutes and a bunch of Corporation whiners. This whole experience was shaping up badly.

"Okay," N'Doro said over the radio. He popped the lock on the door and a whoosh of stale air let me know that the little pirate craft wasn't exactly equipped for intergalactic travel. Big Red avoided the rough and sharp edges and the door closed behind her.

I turned to Spray-gun. "Now what?" I asked.

"Whaddya mean?" he said indignantly. "Why look at me? This whole operation has been one fucking disaster! How the hell do I know what to do? He's your First Officer," he pointed out. He tried to rub his face, but the helmet was in the way. He took it off and I saw that he wasn't half bad to look at.

None of this sounded very reassuring to the folks on the floor behind the counter, and I thought I could hear the gentle heave of quiet weeping back there. At least they were keeping the noise level down. And maybe the Corp whiner had eaten a slug of friendly fire.

I had run out of ideas, not that I'd had any great ones lately anyway, and Spray-gun was clearly at the end of his rope, too. I wondered what led someone into a life of piracy. I think I would have asked him if the airlock door hadn't suddenly jerked open.

"Lookee here!" Big Red cried. She was propping up the inert form of N'Doro in front of the threshold. She had his sidearm buckled around her ample waist.

"Oh, no you don't!" I said as Spray-gun made a move toward the door. I had the little Glock aimed at his face. "Drop the weapon," I ordered.

He just stood there. "Does it get any worse?" he asked with resignation, then let the gun clatter to the floor.

Big Red left N'Doro's body on the floor of the shuttle and stepped over the threshold panting. Spray-gun couldn't take his eyes off her.

I heard whimpers from behind the counter and realized I'd had enough of the whole thing. "You!" I said to Big Red. "Is he dead?" I asked, pointing my weapon at N'Doro.

She shook her head. "Naw, I just knocked him out." She was still looking at Spray-gun. I could almost hear the violins as they locked their eyes on one another. It's always boring when you're not a participant.

"Okay, so you came back for true love," I sighed, "now let's get to work. Come on out of there," I said to the whimperers and the remaining women. They crawled out, businessmen last. The women seemed a little disoriented and the men were clearly in shock. I told the two moonstruck lovers to count and identify the dead.

"Two each," Big Red said in a dreamy voice. "Isn't that romantic?"

"Three, Beautiful," Spray-gun corrected her gently. "I had three."

I sighed again and ushered everyone onto the speedcraft, keeping a close watch on Spray-gun, not that anyone could watch him closer than Big Red. It was a very tight fit. Counting the unconscious N'Doro, there were thirteen of us on a craft designed to hold four. The ship was extremely small and the air was so bad it nauseated me to breathe through my nose, so I didn't. I closed the airlock door.

When we disengaged, my old shuttle blew like popcorn in a microwave, and I set the speedcraft controls on a course for Mare Tranq. But I didn't radio the authorities. Instead, I spent a couple of stifling hours thinking about the plastic material that had sealed the pirate craft to the *Linda Rae*. In sufficient quantities, it could have probably sealed the whole breach in the hull and saved the shuttle. Oh, well.

I looked around at the sardines in my present tin. "What am I going to do with you all?" I asked, more to myself than to any of them.

Admiralty law would normally expect me to bring Spray-gun in on piracy charges and prosecute N'Doro for mutiny. But the way I was feeling, I just wanted to get everyone out of my hair and get some rest. Besides, I was going to have to explain the loss of my shuttle and their cargo to the Corporation. And there was the matter of the dead, two ladies and three pirates. Oh, and did I mention that the punishment for both piracy and mutiny was death? Is that what I wanted for Spray-gun and N'Doro? Well, N'Doro, maybe. . .

By the time we got to Mare Tranq, my nose had grown used to the stench, the whiners were all quietly unconscious thanks to Big Red and her two remaining ladies, N'Doro was begging for mercy and Spray-gun was making wedding plans.

"Can I interrupt your bridal shower for just one moment?" I asked. He looked up with a goofy grin. He had been drawing pictures of the cake. I was amazed and slightly revolted to learn that his real name was Lester Snipely. Even Spray-gun was a better name than that. "What do you propose I do with you once we land?"

"Uh, well, you could just let us go," he suggested amiably. "Red and I want to get married and start our own business. The girls will work for us and I think we can make a go of things in Mare Tranq." This from a pirate who had been responsible for five deaths a few hours ago. Somehow the thought of them running a pleasure palace wasn't too far off the wall, though. How much damage could they do there?

"And what about you?" I asked N'Doro. N'Doro was now a willing slave, begging and groveling at every cramped and smelly turn. I really wanted to execute him.

"Anything, Captain," he said, "anything."

Anything can mean a lot.

The Corporation authorities at Mare Tranq kept me busy. We went over my story at least a hundred times, but as there was no conflicting testimony, and as I had a dozen witnesses, they finally had to accept my version of things, which fingered the dead pirates as ringleaders, with Spray-gun as their unwilling captive and N'Doro playing a minor hero in the proceedings.

At Mare Tranq, Big Red became Mrs. Lester Snipely in a lavish ceremony. She had two beautiful young bridesmaids and N'Doro was the best man. As I remarked at the time, I guess he was the best they could do. I was the maid of honor and caught the bouquet, too. Lucky me.

They put me back on the earth to Mare Tranq run again, only in a nice, new shuttle. The Corporation assigned me a new First Officer, too - a handsome young woman who took her duties seriously and spied on me whenever she thought I wasn't looking. I guess the Corporation never really believed my version of events, but there was nothing they could do. After all, I was the captain, and by Admiralty law, I could dispose of the situation as I saw fit.

N'Doro became captain of another shuttle, the *Dory Hall*, on the Earth to Sagan run. I see him once in a while, whenever I need a favor. Or whenever I need information and a partner. And someday we might fly together again, you never know. You see, I kept Lester's speedcraft and every once in a while, when N'Doro tells me there's going to be a large shipment of something tasty with little to nothing in the way of passengers, I put it to good use and the pirates strike again.

Language Barrier

Who doesn't love a cuddly kitty?

I hadn't really wanted a cat on the trip - I never asked for one, and I knew how much extra trouble a small animal could be, especially one that wouldn't stay put in a cage like, say, an iguana or something.

I knew about iguanas. Clean, quiet, primeval-looking. Not much in the way of cuddly, but sometimes you just want something you can talk to who won't answer you back or come equipped with an attitude.

Not, for example, like a cat. Having a cat on board was almost as bad as having another person. You had to be careful about your habits, remember to feed it, do that whole litter-box routine - it was just a major-sized hassle. And for what? So it would turn its nose up at you and refuse to let you pet it.

It blinked its golden eyes at me and just stared, several pounds of cat muscle in a velvety black coat. It was indeed beautiful, and even if I didn't have any real use for it, its decorative qualities might excuse its inconvenience. Besides, it was a paying passenger. Or cargo, whatever.

Okay, Cat, I thought, resigned to its presence. There was really no sense in talking aloud to myself this early in the trip. The time would come when the craving for conversation would steer me to my own slightly schizophrenic gabfest. But not yet.

I checked the control panels for the umpteenth time since lift-off. Everything was fine. Everything would be fine. Trips from the station at Southwest Terminal to the Biosphere Ventures Domes outside of the government facility at Mars Colony were now almost routine. After all, we had shuttled nearly six thousand colonists over the last couple of years. The Domes were a thriving city now, expanding like a fungus over the surface of the Red Planet.

I guess I could have made my living in some more orderly and sane fashion, say as a nude dancer at a sex club in Mare Tranquillitatis. Shuttle operators tended toward short lives, burned out at the end by the long silence of the trip and the stress. But I liked the combination of absolute peaceful quiet punctuated periodically by the life-threatening horror of take-off and landing. The extremes suited me. And this was long before the Corporation demanded a co-pilot, so I was very much alone for most of these trips. My association with the gorgeous N'Doro was still an undreamed of pleasure.

A cat. Okay, maybe it would work. But if the damned thing became too much of a nuisance, it was going into the regenerator with the rest of the trash.

I got out my favorite book. It was my favorite on that particular trip, anyway. Each trip I read something new. I know, I could have had movies, games, music, holographic images, you name it, for entertainment. Practically anything the inventive geniuses at Sony and Toshiba and Apogee could come up with. But I liked the idea of books. And I particularly liked the pictures in my head, much more vivid and real than anything a programmer could dream up. Of course, the Corporation shrinks thought I had a screw loose, but doesn't every shuttle pilot?

Back then, the trip from Earth to Mars took twenty-four days. This sounds like a long time, especially since it only took two minutes to go by hub from Southwest in California to Sord L'Abbaye in France. But while there were advanced travel methods between the large hubs on Earth, space was a different story.

The hubs, located in or near major cities of North America, Europe, Asia, the Indian sub-continent, Australia, Africa and Central America, could whisk groups of people from one place to another in minutes. The millennium war isolated South America, and space travel, while possible, wasn't anything like the efficient mass transit available everywhere else on Earth.

My shuttle, the *Linda Rae*, was carrying almost four hundred people on that particular trip, most of them families of four to six persons each. This lot was destined for the mining village at the far end of the Domes. They had all been paid handsomely and had gone through some minor biological modifications to make life in the Domes a little easier. Colonization then was still a strictly volunteer enterprise in those days, with thousands on the waiting lists.

Shuttle passengers usually elected to make the trip in a sleeplike trance, to avoid the monotony of twenty-four days in space. But there were always a couple of hardy souls who wanted to experience every moment of the ride. They usually regretted this choice bitterly at take-off, and once again upon landing.

Take-off had been a little shaky. I got everything up and running just fine, but as usual there were a hundred computer glitches that I had to use the manual override on. We swung wide, then back again in a stomach-churning motion which made me sweat and left the two gentlemen who had elected to forego twilight sleep heaving up their breakfasts. I saw them through the plexiglas window, but paid no attention. The craft yawed dangerously during atmospheric escape and I had visions of us slamming into the Rio Norte mountain range.

We lost about two or three shuttles a year to take-off and landing problems. You'd think the designers would get busy and iron out a few of the big ones, but with potential colonists practically beating the doors down, the Corporation just racked it up to 'acceptable losses' and moved on. Beside, who would you get to work the problem? Everyone with any brains worked for the big corporations and space travel, even to the established colonies on the moon and Mars, was not a priority.

I was just getting comfy with my book and the cat had perched a few feet away and was at least pretending to sleep when I felt rather than heard the two ambulatory passengers attempting to pry open my door.

I jumped up in a panic and the cat disappeared, scuttling into some corner or other. I grabbed my weapon, a clumsy old-fashioned Glock stingray, and pointed it at the sealed edge of my doorframe where a long metal object was being worked through.

"What the fuck you guys think you're doing?" I screamed. My hands shook as I found the trigger of the gun and pressed lightly, too lightly to fire but hard enough to know I could do it if I had to.

The intruders were the same two guys who had thrown up on take-off. They'd had enough time to get cleaned up and either get angry over something or go completely crazy. I didn't know or care which. It was strictly forbidden to have any contact with the colonists, ostensibly for their protection as their immune systems were altered slightly to accommodate the prevailing dangers of the air in the Domes. I liked it that way. I always felt it was for my own protection, too. Protection from mindless chatter, unnecessary noise, and self-righteous twaddle.

Now it was also for protection from a large metal bar which had successfully loosened my door. Bony white fingers grasped the door and pulled on it. It opened. It wasn't really designed to withstand an assault of any kind.

One old dude brandished the bar. I took aim as the other one screamed, and I pressed more firmly on the trigger. The gun vibrated in my hand as a stream of something - some kind of ray or quanta or particle, I don't know, I'm not a physicist - shot out and struck the bar-brandisher in the chest. He flew backward out of my space and into the passenger area.

The other one, the screamer, turned his attention to his fallen comrade and bent to help him, babbling in some tongue foreign to me.

I jumped through the jagged doorway and aimed the weapon at the second man. "You!" I shouted. "Get away from him!" I motioned with the gun, but Babblemouth didn't hear or care. Or maybe he didn't understand. He looked up at me and tears streamed down his face. I pushed him with my foot and he backed away. I kept the gun on him as I examined the one I had shot.

He was okay. He was breathing and from the little scorch marks on his shirt, I could tell that I had hit the target perfectly, but since I had the weapon on its very lowest setting, there was no harm done. The old guy had just fainted with the impact of the weapon stream.

His buddy didn't know that, though, and wept audibly. It got to me. I like absolute quiet, remember? And these two had just got my heart pounding so loudly I could hardly stand it. I took a deep breath and motioned for Babblemouth to stand up. He did so, still whimpering.

I kept the gun on Babblemouth as I bent over the other one and shook him a bit to revive him. He groaned and sat up and rubbed his arm. "Jeeze, lady," he said. "You didn't have to shoot me!"

"That's Captain Sullivan to you," I said.

Babblemouth went nuts and started jabbering like a wild man, leaping toward the other one. A motion of my gun kept him in place.

"Okay, buddy," I said to the recovering one, "sit up nice and we'll have a little talk. And tell your pal there to shut up."

He said something to Babblemouth who promptly went quiet, then he turned to me. "There's really no need for the weapon, Miss." His voice was calm and dignified and very persuasive, but I kept the Glock on him anyway. I didn't say anything, trying to regain my sense of calm.

"I know this looks bad," he continued, "but it's not what you think. If you'll just listen to me. . ."

I saw the wary look on Babblemouth's face. I didn't like it. I motioned them both into my quarters with the gun. I kept a few paces behind them, and turned the dial up a bit on the Glock. If I had to blast them, they would stay down for a while.

I put Babblemouth in the recliner and the other one in the console chair, and tied them in with tape from the repair box on the wall. Once I was satisfied that they couldn't get away, I perched on the low table.

"Okay, guys," I said in a friendly tone, "what's the story?" Whatever it was, it would be an interesting break. I wasn't sure what I would do with them, though. I mean, I probably had to deliver all the bodies at the other end, Geneva Convention rules and all, but they didn't necessarily have to be alive.

"I am John Huntington Scharf," the persuasive one said, "and this is my colleague, Dr. Antonio Romero." He gestured toward Babblemouth. Dr. Babblemouth.

"I deeply regret what we have been forced to do here. You see, it just seemed like a good opportunity." He smiled, an engaging smile for a guy who had to be seventy if he was a day. I knew he had to be somebody important. They don't send out seventy-year-old colonists unless there is a compelling reason to do so. This guy, and his pal for that matter, had to be big shots of some kind.

"Opportunity for what?" I asked. "This is a shuttle to the Mars colony. You are colonists. What other sort of opportunities did you have in mind?" Something clicked, but I pushed the thought out of my mind. These guys were too old to be thinking of things like subduing a female shuttle pilot for a few days of slap and tickle. Well, they looked too old, anyway.

"Maybe we got off to a bad start," Scharf said. "Maybe we should start over."

"Maybe without a pry bar this time," I agreed. "And with you two where I can keep an eye on you. I hope you're comfy because this is where you'll be spending the next twenty-three days." I said that last part just for the effect it would have on them, but they both smiled.

"So Dr. Romero understands English?" I asked. I had to be faster with these two.

"But of course, Señorita," he replied, grinning and bowing his head a bit in a courtly gesture.

I rolled my eyes – There was no getting these two to call me Captain.

"Dr. Romero is a linguist," Scharf explained, "and I have studied astronomy. We are both retired, but we keep busy." Colonizing Mars would keep anyone busy, I thought, especially a pair of seventy-year-olds.

"So start at the beginning. You two didn't just get bored after take-off and decide to poke around with a stick." Their stick, the metal pry bar, was still lying in the doorway where Scharf had dropped it. I jumped down from the table and scooped it up. It was a nifty device - a real pry bar, made for the purpose, not some stray piece of junk from the passenger cabin floor. They had planned to break in to my quarters.

Scharf shot a glance at Romero, allowed the cat to settle on his lap, then told me their story. They were just puttering around on Earth, in Buenos Aires, as a matter of fact, at the old radio telescope there. Scharf had been a visiting professor or something in the old days and had retired to a part of the world not easily accessible anymore. He liked the idea of living a sort of stone age existence, where a tiny home computer and some sort of gasoline-driven cart were the only modern luxuries available.

"I took my car up the hill every morning to the telescope and continued to send signals and record my observations. Old habits are difficult to break," he explained. "But it wasn't until I met Romero that things began to fall into place."

"It was my good fortune to meet Dr. Scharf," Romero picked up where Scharf had left off, "and we began to develop a project together. At first, it was just coffee and conversation in the park every morning, but soon Dr. Scharf gave me a tour of the observatory and showed me his work. I, too, had been retired for a while, but had never lost my academic habits. I was very impressed with his ideas, but I could see a different application for them, one that would incorporate my work, too."

A linguist and an astronomer, I thought. What were they going to do, talk to the stars?

They waited for me to say something, but I had lost the habit of conversation after my first couple of shuttle trips. Scharf petted the cat and resumed.

"It became clear that communication with species other than our own was not only possible, but necessary," he said. "We spent many days and long evenings working on the methods to be used."

"Wait a minute," I broke in, "we already have inter-species communication. You know, dolphins, primates, that sort of thing." And everyone also knew that it didn't make any difference in the scheme of things. Someone figured out that it took more to communicate with a dolphin than teaching it English, and made the next great leap. But the results were not what everyone expected. Communication was achieved on one level, that is, we could sort of talk back and forth, but the way dolphins saw the world and their own existence was so different from anything we as humans had ever imagined, that real communication was simply not possible. And it was the dolphins who gave up trying. It was even worse with primates - but the phenomenon was dubbed "The Dolphin Paradigm" and the name stuck. Inter-species communication was no longer the ticket to a brilliant academic career.

"Yes, that sort of communication was a great disappointment," Romero agreed. "But it was not the end of my work. I continued to experiment with communicatory methods beyond language, and found that as long as the individual species' worldview roughly paralleled that of our own, true communication was possible. I had my greatest success with dogs," he admitted modestly.

Dogs! I remembered. So this was the guy who made the talking dogs possible. Well, the dogs couldn't really talk, since their vocal anatomy wasn't conducive to human speech, but they sure could understand human language. It was weird. Once you communicated with something, it didn't seem so foreign. Communication was a humanizing sort of thing - one of the reasons it didn't work with the dolphins was that they were just too far from human in the way they thought. But dogs thought pretty much like people. Or maybe vice versa.

"When I met Dr. Scharf," Romero continued, "we were just a couple of old duffers messing about with what we used to do, hanging on to the tail end of our careers, living quietly in the backwater of the world. But the spark was still there. Our age had not diminished our capabilities, although it was impossible to generate any interest in our work or to obtain any funding. So we made a simple decision. If our work reached a point where we must leave the observatory and actually go out into space to continue it, we would do so, by whatever means we could."

Romero said this with finality and Scharf said nothing, but continued to stroke the sleeping cat in his lap.

"So you decided to volunteer as colonists?" I asked. It seemed like a pretty dramatic step for a couple of old researchers to take, not to mention the companies usually wanted younger, breeding-age families. Colonies could live just fine without retired old guys cluttering up the place. "How'd you get accepted?"

Scharf grinned. He seemed to have all his teeth, but the image of the toothless aged was really just an outdated stereotype anyway. No one actually lost their teeth anymore, not for a couple of hundred years. "We lied," he said. "We told them we were younger and had the forged papers to prove it."

"Didn't they look at you?" I asked incredulously. "Couldn't they tell?"

"It's the Corporation bureaucracy," Romero explained. "No one talks to anyone else in person. As long as our computer records matched, the only people who actually saw us were the medics. And by the time we went in for medical alterations, we were already signed up. The Corporation thought they were getting a couple of very experienced and academically qualified young men."

"Well, younger than us, anyway," Scharf said. "I think we told them we were thirty-five. It seemed like a good age."

"So then what?" I asked. "What were you going to do?"

"Well, you might have already guessed that we weren't going to work in the mining domes of Mars," Scharf continued. "We needed to get off-planet, and since our space program is limited to the Moon and Mars shuttles, your craft was the most likely for our purposes. How was I to know that it would be so difficult to overpower you? You look like just a slip of a girl." Scharf shook his head sadly. "We were so close." His hand rested on the cat's glossy black fur.

"When you shot Dr. Scharf," Romero said, his voice cracking, "I thought you had killed him. I was devastated. The work gone, our chances gone, everything gone." His eyes watered up a bit. He was an emotional sort.

"Wait a minute," I said. "Tell me exactly what your work is. Maybe I can help you in some way." I knew that I had one job as far as the Corporation was concerned, and that was to deliver a shuttle-load of colonists and then get my cute little ass back as fast as possible and do it all over again. But I wanted to know what it was that was so important that a couple of septuagenarians would try to hijack a shuttle craft with three hundred and eighty four other people on it, counting myself.

Scharf and Romero exchanged those weird glances again. I guess they had been communicating with each other for so long that they didn't really need to say anything anymore. But Scharf spoke up. "We need to get to a point just between the orbits of Mars and Jupiter, I have the coordinates. I thought we'd be able to fly the shuttle there, do what we have to, and then send it back in the right direction. It might take a couple of extra days, and you'd have a bunch of hungry, angry people awake before you landed at the Domes, but no one would be seriously hurt."

"Why?" What the heck was out in the middle of empty space?

"We can't tell you," Romero said.

"Then you stay here for the next twenty-three days," I snapped. Only I didn't like the idea much. I didn't want them around, taking up space in my quarters for that long. Besides, they had to eat and everything. I just didn't want the hassle.

And every day they spent in my quarters was another chance for them to break free and overpower me. Plus I had a whole ship load of people to think about. I made a quick decision, one I hoped I wouldn't regret.

I took the emergency injector out of the tool kit and shot them both up with enough twilight sleep to keep them out - and out of my hair - for the rest of the trip. Then I dragged their inert bodies back out to the passenger area, dumped them into a couple of recliner beds, and wished them nightie-night.

I repaired my door, fed the cat, and went to sleep.

I spent the rest of the trip reading up on the space between Mars and Jupiter, but frankly, there wasn't much to read about. There was nothing out there, the companies weren't interested in exploration beyond the only habitable and exploitable planets, and no one except Romero and Scharf had the slightest interest in the place.

When I got near Mars and started preparing for the landing, I decided to do something that could cost me my job. I hid the sleeping doctors in my quarters. They weren't cut out for colony life anyway. They were old, for crying out loud.

The Domes appeared first on my instruments, then on my observation screen, and I went into the landing dance and hoped for the best. I didn't crash the shuttle and everyone on board survived so I guess it turned out okay.

The crews came in to revive the colonists and clean the shuttle, and this was the part where I usually went to one of the hot spots to unwind for a while before the return trip. Only this time I stayed on board and didn't let them mess around in my quarters. I waited until my successful, if jolting, take-off to get the old guys up. They were bleary-eyed, confused, and hungry, so I showed them the shower then I fixed a meal.

I explained that I had failed to deliver them to Mars. I thought they might be angry, but they weren't, they were just glad to still be alive and kicking.

Maybe I was glad to have a couple of nut cases on board, gladder still that the ship was empty except for the three of us and the cat. At any rate, I invited them to expand on their less-than-satisfactory explanation of why they had gone to such extraordinary lengths to get out to a spot in the middle of absolute nowhere. You see, I had it within my limited power to actually take them to that spot on the return trip. It would be stretching the fuel situation a bit, and the craft was pretty old and worn to be taking joyrides through the solar system, and I would almost certainly be fired for it, but it was possible.

I just needed a good reason.

I guess I have to admit that I didn't believe them at first. The tale they told me was so improbable that I put it right up there with stories about flying saucers and little green men. But I was curious, too. I mean, what could it hurt to just check it out?

So I set the coordinates manually and we headed out away from the familiar Earth-Mars path toward a point in empty space.

Scharf had practically adopted the cat, whom he called "Twinky" on account of what he thought were its twinkling eyes, but it was Romero who spent hours trying to talk to the little beast. They were happy and excited and kept jabbering at each other in half-snatches of English, Spanish, and what have you. It was enough to get on my nerves, but I kept telling myself that a little noise and conversation was probably good for me.

We reached the point in four days. I had turned off the radio connection with the Corporation so I wouldn't have to listen to them telling me my craft had deviated from the standard path. They wouldn't care after a while anyway, as it was an empty return flight. They would chalk it up to instrument malfunction or pilot error and send up another old bucket to take its place on the run.

I looked out through the observation screen and didn't see anything. I didn't know how to tell the guys. I didn't want to see their disappointment. I had already offered to take them back to Earth after our little journey, but they kept insisting that it wouldn't be necessary. As much as I was convinced that we would find nothing out there, I was also scared they might be right.

The first transmissions scared the shit out of me. I screamed when the voice communicator crackled on and a whining, sing-song voice asked for "Rrrrowwmeeerowww."

I put him on. He spoke in the same whining voice. Scharf was right there with him, dancing around excitedly. Even the cat was alert. It had jumped up on the console and was adding its two-cents worth of yowls to the babble of conversation.

I flipped on the observation screen and gasped. The ship was unlike anything I had ever seen. It was large and oddly-shaped, iridescent and seemed to pulse somehow.

Dr. Scharf turned to me and managed to tear me away from the screen. "I said the captain of the other ship is requesting permission to take us aboard. As captain of this ship, do you agree to it?" I nodded. Yeah, sure, whatever.

Dr. Romero took me by the shoulders and got my attention. "As captain, first contact is your privilege." At last. He called me Captain. Almost.

I shook my head. "N-no, you guys go ahead," I stammered, "It's your project."

They both grinned. It was what they wanted more than anything.

The shuttle craft shuddered as the big alien ship locked on. Then the hiss of the airlock told me we had company. Dr. Romero stood at attention in front of the airlock door, Dr. Scharf by his side with Twinky in his arms. I flipped the door switch and stood behind them.

The creatures were large, mammalian-looking, covered in dark, glossy fur. I could see no expression on their faces, although they had two eyes, a nose, and a mouth. They walked gracefully upright and carried some sort of weapons or maybe ceremonial things in fur-covered hands not that much different from my own.

They went directly to Dr. Scharf and bowed. Dr. Romero spoke to them in their own language and they bowed to him, too.

They saw me and gave a little half-bow. Romero must have told them I was the captain or something, and they presented me with a scroll. I bowed back.

Then Romero turned to me and gave me a hug. "We're going with them," he said. "Can you get back alright?"

I nodded. Dr. Scharf put Twinky down and hugged me too. "Thank you, my dear," he said kindly. "You have done humankind a wonderful service."

Twinky walked to the aliens and they prostrated themselves before him. "Is he a god?" I asked. The cat yowled and they rose.

Romero laughed. "No, but he's going to be a translator, and that's a very important position. When you get back, give the scroll to the Corporation president. We'll be in touch, you know. Just keep an eye on the communicator screens."

I watched them stand formally in the airlock, all of them, and I waved as the door shut. The locks hissed and screeched and the shuttle craft lurched, then they were gone.

I set the course for the shuttle docking bay on Earth and spent the next twenty-eight days thinking about what had happened and trying to make my food last.

Landing was worse than usual, and I crashed somewhere to the south of the docking bay.

When I woke up in the hospital, the autonurses were going full blast and I could see my condition in the monitor. I was still alive, but my feet had been burned off and the new ones were still little weird things in the nutrient solution. I wasn't going to be walking anywhere for a while.

The Corporation sent a representative to find out what the hell I had been doing on the return trip. I told them I had equipment malfunctions and ended up way off course. I didn't mention Romero, Scharf, the aliens, or Twinky. The Corporation believed me, since the shuttle had been totaled in the crash landing.

The scroll was lost.

When I tell this story, usually in some crappy bar for the price of a cheap drink, most of my listeners chalk it up to the deranged ramblings of a shuttle-rat. I used to show them my feet, pretty as a child's, a little mis-matched to the rest of me, as proof. And I waited for Dr. Scharf or Dr. Romero to get in touch with me. They didn't know I couldn't find their coordinates anymore and that the scroll was never delivered.

I eventually went back to my Corporation job, but not until I had spent a year on sick leave in the abandoned observatory waiting for them to find me. Every time we make contact or set foot on a new world, I still look for them. But they must be long dead by now.

We never did make contact with anything that looked like big cats, except once, but that's another story.

Cause and Effect

A Mare Inebrium Story by Kate Thornton

Mare Inebrium Universe created by Dan Hollifield

The Mare Inebrium, a bar on Bethdish, a planet in the fertile imagination of Dan Hollifield, Editor of the long-running science fiction ezine, Aphelion, *has been the setting for a plethora of stories by a diverse collection of talented writers. I love writing stories set there. Along with Stinky Puffer's on Cernan, it's my kinda joint.*

This story has been modified slightly from its original form due to gender issues with the humanoids and the D'rhissh.

The first time I ended up in the Mare Inebrium, a spaceport bar on Bethdish, about sixteen secs outta my usual stomping ground, it was to celebrate the weirdest event of my life.

You've probably heard about people who find things by lucky coincidence, but let me tell you right now, there ain't no such thing. Everything has a cause and is an effect, and if you don't believe me, ask any quantum physicist you know, except maybe Tom Wilcox, whose ideas are so far out that the Quantum Physics Guild is thinking of branding him a heretic, a particle physicist, and throwing him out. But that's another story.

Anyway, I used to run a contract shuttle out of Mare Tranquillitatis on the Earth's moon. This was years ago, way before interstellar contact. Hell, we had just had our first interplanetary contact in those days, and set up a few Mars colonies just for the profit. When the Outside finally broke through our defenses and made what Earthers refer to as "First Contact," it was a jolt and a half to discover what all was out there. Who all was out there.

My shuttle, the *Linda Rae*, was a rusted out bucket of wire and stray electrons, but I kept her running and even managed, through shrewd business and even shrewder smuggling, to save a few credits and buy a larger, newer craft. This I also named the *Linda Rae*. Okay, I named all my ships *Linda Rae*. It was an aberration, I guess.

I guess I'm telling you all this history because I want you to know that as far as my piloting skills go, I was a shuttle rat long before most of you were hatched outta your egg sacs, or whatever.

Anyway, I was on Mars when the Outside contacted, and I signed on immediately with the first exploration/diplomatic crews, not as a diplomat, of course, as a pilot. In exchange, I got a fancy uniform, a fancier spacecraft, and a course at knife and fork school so's I could figure out how not to cause an intergalactic incident with my big mouth.

After a stint in the antipiracy fleet, I stayed on as a Corporation pilot in the Diplomatic Corps. I didn't do so bad for the first few years, you know, saw the universe and everything, managed to keep outta trouble most of the time.

Then I met It. Well, it wasn't really a face-to-face meeting, it was more like a mind-to-mind meeting. It was unlike anyone, anything, I had ever seen before. At first, it was just another high-ranking passenger, a diplomat, an ambassador on home leave. I kept away from my VIP cargo, mostly 'cause they usually gave me the willies. We're talking creatures from Out There and Beyond, know what I mean?

But there was something about it. It was all swathed up in a protective suit, and I couldn't tell at first if it was actually as big as the suit or if it was a complete habitat or something. I mean, it was about ten feet long and six feet tall. That would be one big entity, you know?

Anyway, it could talk to me through a translator, and the voice was all silky and slippery and sweet, like a peppermint after it's been in your mouth for a while. We had a long way to go, all the way back to its home planet, and since it wanted to talk, I thought why not? I should have known better.

It told me stories of a place of unimaginable beauty, where the sands glowed in the protected city, and of the rest of the planet, open to offworlders like myself. It spoke fondly of its father and how it had followed in his footsteps to its present position as ambassador. I guess I musta fallen in love with it.

Knife and fork school had not prepared me for that. Nothing had. I had imagined falling in love with a handsome male of either my species or some other quasi-human species, but not, well, whatever this was. I spoke plainly to it, confessed my feelings, and waited to see what would happen. I was so far gone, I didn't even think what it must look like under the protective suit. I guess I didn't even care. I was already making mental plans to retire from the Corporation and go to live with it in that sacred city, if the family agreed.

It was quiet for the rest of the trip. I sweated it out, hoping I hadn't insulted it. I tried to speak with it, maybe apologize or something, but it wouldn't see me. I spent the rest of the flight with my stomach twisted up like a Brashqueath's hairdo.

When we touched down outside the sacred city, I tried once again to speak to it, but I was dismissed curtly. I lifted off with tears in my eyes, the white form of its protective habitat like a royal tent shimmering on the sands below me. I had been to Bethdish lots of times, even out to the sacred city once, but never with an ache in my heart.

Since I was on Bethdish, I flew to the big spaceport and blindly stumbled into the nearest bar. It was the Mare Inebrium.

There was a celebration in progress when I arrived. Creatures from all over the universe were imbibing and Max, the bartender was busy. A pretty waitress who turned out to be Max's girlfriend Trixie recommended the house specialty and I was too heartbroken to protest.

"So what's the party about?" I asked when she brought me a Zombie Cocktail. I took a sip and felt my hormones leveling upwards, easing the depression I had felt since I had left the sacred city.

"It's him," she said, pointing to a giant scorpion about thirty feet long. He wore the sash and insignia of a diplomat and appeared to be dancing with a vaguely humanoid person dressed in feathers. Or maybe growing feathers, I don't know.

"What is he?" I asked. I had long ago learned that just because something looks like a giant scorpion, that doesn't mean it is one.

"He's a *D'rhissh*," Trixie explained. "He's a regular here, knows a lot of really good stories. But today's story is the best. He's going to be a grandfather or something."

"Wow, that's great," I said, feeling much better and ordering another Zombie. I lifted my glass to the giant bug and toasted him. He came over and waved his eyestalks at me, a friendly gesture, I'm told. "Congratulations!" I offered.

"I thank you," he said in a rich, mellifluous voice that had a little bit of the familiar about it. He peered at me for a minute, then his pincers began to quiver. "It - it's you!" he said. "Everyone," he turned to the crowded bar, "it's she! It's she!" He began dancing around me as I was showered with drinks and good wishes. I finished off a third Zombie and passed out.

When I awoke, it was in an Arabian Nights sort of room right off the main bar. Trixie was standing over me with a cool washcloth and Max was patting my wrist. Kazsh-ak Tier, the *D'rhissh* diplomat, was agitatedly pacing back and forth, his stinger whipping the air like a nervous cat's tail.

"You must save her," he was saying to Trixie. "She is now of my family."

"She's okay," Trixie assured the *D'rhissh*. "She just had a little too much to drink, that's all."

"What's going on?" I asked. My head was a little mixed up, probably the effects of Zombies, aliens and stress, a killer combination.

"Kazsh-ak tells us you're the parent of his grandchildren," Max said. "Said you and his offspring made the Pact during the flight out."

"What?" My diplomatic skills, such as they were, failed me completely. "What?"

"Kazshi-annh Tier is my offspring," the giant scorpion said. "And is the one you have just delivered to our sacred city. Did you not profess undying love for Kazshi-annh Tier?"

"I-uh, uh," I stammered. "I didn't know its name," I blurted out, "Was it in a large plastic tent?"

"That was the protective suit," Trixie explained. "Kazsh-ak's offspring took over as ambassador when he retired. According to their custom, when one professes love for a *D'rhissh*, it is then at liberty to release eggs. They go out into that desert that surrounds the *D'rhissh* city with several of their kind, for the physical side of things - *D'rhissh* sex takes too long to explain. What it all boils down to is - Looks like you're gonna be a mommy," she said with a grin. "Or a daddy. Or a something."

Max whistled. "You are one brave gal," he said admiringly. "You know, the mate runs the risk of being eaten by the egg-dropper in this courting stuff. It must have really liked you to forgo that particular pleasure."

"Ah, like my own dear mate," Kazsh-ak exclaimed. "Well, now that we are to be family, please let me buy you a drink my dear. We must become better acquainted."

I let them all lead me through the bar to a large chair as dozens of creatures applauded and made approving noises, some accompanied by interesting colors and odors.

I learned that Kazshi-annh would not be expecting me to play any role in the conception or development of the young. Someone of its own species would be filling those roles. I felt relief that child support for a couple of hundred young scorpions would not be part of my responsibility.

"When can I see Kazshi-annh?" I asked, wondering if there would still be a chance for it to devour me.

Kazsh-ak set a pincer gently on my back and rubbed it lightly in an affectionate gesture. "I am sorry, my dear. It is not our custom. You will not see Kazshi-annh again. I know this must pain one of your species, but it is our way, Cookie Sullivan- rhieashh."

I let this bit of news sink in, then did what I knew was expected of me. I embraced my new father-in-law to the extent that our differing anatomies would permit, and I bought the house a round.

There's Always a Reason

A Mare Inebrium Story by Kate Thornton

Mare Inebrium Universe created by Dan Hollifield

Several of Cookie's stories were set in the Mare Inebrium, a watering place frequented by, well, everything.

It wasn't just the blasting headache I had, the kind where you think you might feel better if you either opened your skull and ran a garden hose full of cold water through it or just blew the sucker off with a moderate explosive. No, my melancholy mood went much deeper than the mere physical discomforts caused by an inordinate amount of Toshiban joy juice.

I had a good time during the joy juice - don't get me wrong. Even shuttle pilots of the female persuasion in the poverty zone can still have a very good time, especially if it includes pressure casks of illicit liquor and charming companions of the opposite sex who have been space borne just a wee bit too long for anything even remotely normal to happen.

But all good things eventually mutate into boredom or headaches.

I popped a nasal cap and inhaled the drug. I didn't like taking painkillers, even the kind that just ironed out your spasming blood vessels and restored your brain function to at least that of a Martian land mollusk. The headache disappeared instantly, but that lingering feeling of sadness defied the chemicals.

"Hey, Captain!" It was the grating voice of my sometimes co-pilot, N'Doro. His usually silky tones were roughed up with the Toshiban juice and a night of raucous laughter and bawdy songs. He had a lovely voice, but couldn't carry a tune with both hands and a bucket. No matter, he was tall, handsome, and dumb enough to fly with me on my old spit and glue rust bucket.

"Captain, I got us a cargo!" His black eyes gleamed in the polished jet of his skin. They didn't gleam with intelligence, just eagerness and excitement.

"Swell," I said, thinking of the previous evening's offers. I coulda carried anything from endangered baby aquatics outta the deep rivers on Mars to cigarettes and nylons for the cribs at Mare Tranq. Yeah, right. "C'mon, N'Doro," I patiently explained. "We don't have a license, remember? We barely have a ship, remember? And whatever offers we get, we can't take because we are grounded, remember?"

N'Doro's handsome face fell. "Oh, yeah."

I sighed. I had been running junk cargo on the *Linda Rae* ever since my father went to the big spaceport in the sky after either a heroic adventure involving pirates and a princess or else getting caught with someone else's wife in the cargo hold of a freighter docked at Mare Tranq. But all good things come to an end, or at least a detour, and the authorities had refused to renew the registration on the *Linda Rae*, had stripped me of my pilot's license, and had grounded N'Doro as well. This was more than a little setback. If I didn't think of something fast, our careers - not to mention food supply - would be at an end.

"Look," I said, thinking as fast as I could with most of my brain circuits on hold and the rest getting a busy signal, "why don't we just look around here and see if we can find any work. You're big and strong, N'Doro," I watched his pearly grin flash slowly into full lumens, "and I'll bet we come across something before lunch. So just relax, guy, and go play some games." I tossed him a plastic credit - probably my last - and he took up a position at a gaming station.

The planet was Bethdish and the joint we were in was the Mare Inebrium, although I couldn't remember exactly how we came to be there at the local equivalent of seven in the morning. A charming young lady of truly interesting proportions was polishing glasses at the end of the bar while a couple of various offworlders dozed or passed out or were maybe dead in a booth across the way. I know, I know, "offworlders" isn't politically correct these days, I'm supposed to say "planetarily challenged" or something, especially when I'm part of the same description, the lovely Bethdish not exactly being my home world, either.

Max, the bartender from the previous evening, was absent, probably catching a few well-deserved hours of sleep after the wrestling match with that big bulbous thing and those long, boring stories from one of the scorpion guys. I'll say this for the place; it sure had a mixed clientele.

Anyway, there I was, wide awake and slightly worried about how to get the *Linda Rae* out of the local lockup where the authorities had towed her when this guy walks in and sits down next to me.

I don't usually mind company. Even when it is short, squat, and dumpy-looking, with a nose way too big and hair bristling out of its ears, in a pinch I can smile pretty and accept a drink. But when it is also wearing the uniform of a Bethdish Stellar Confiscation Officer, I must draw the line. Only since I didn't have two credits to rub together, I didn't have anything to draw a line with, so I forced myself to smile pretty and waited for the drink and inevitable pickup line.

Forced myself because this was the guy who had taken my *Linda Rae*.

"Hey, Beautiful," he said, loud and hearty in a slightly nasal voice. "Buy you a drink?"

"What, at this hour?" I was dying for a drink.

"Trixie," he said to the girl at the bar. "Bring us couple of frin juices, the real thing this time."

Jeeze, frin juice. It was sweet, delicious, and rare, squeezed from a fruit grown halfway across the galaxy. I was impressed. Maybe things were looking up.

The frin juice arrived and I tried to be cool and sip instead of knocking it back and smacking my lips. The juice was sublime, nourishing, healthy, and delicate and I damn near choked trying to drink it like a lady. I looked at the local authority and calculated just how much of what I might owe him for the frin juice experience. I decided it didn't matter and I would pay up - a debt is a debt.

"So, I understand you're in a bit of a tight spot," he said.

As it was a spot of his making, he understood pretty well. I smiled wanly and nodded. "Uh-huh," I agreed.

"Well, maybe I can help you out a bit." I kept on smiling. I figured something like this might happen. It always does.

"Here's the deal, Prettyface. You and your pal take a little something to the other side of the world for me, and I'll square the license and registration thing."

"Huh?" I said with my usual seven a.m. articulation.

"It's a small package," he explained, "but I don't want it going through the usual checkpoints."

"Wait a minute," I said, "you are the usual checkpoint, in case you hadn't noticed. I mean you've got the uniform and everything." Maybe this was a test.

"Look, even I have a private life sometimes." He looked into my eyes with that curious blue-grey look the humanoid Bethdishers have, and I felt my heart melt. Okay, maybe it was another part of my anatomy, but what's the diff?

"Alright, alright, what's the deal?" I could tell by the pinging sound in the corner that N'Doro was having good luck with his space game, which was good, since the only replays we could afford were the ones he could rack up himself. And if the nice Stellar Confiscation Officer wanted me to do a little something for him in exchange for our licenses and ship, well, something could be worked out. I didn't even know his name, but in cases like this, that could be a good thing.

"My name is Kraygg," he said, and I winced involuntarily. I didn't want to get personally involved, I just wanted to do business and get my ship back. He reached into a pocket and brought out a little box small enough to fit in the palm of his hairy, six-fingered hand. I realized that I liked men with six-fingered hands.

"What is it?" I asked. "And where do you want me to take it?" It sat in his hand like a little animal, small, inquisitive, quivering slightly. Wait a minute, it was just a little box, for crying out loud. What was I thinking?

"It's a psibox, and I want you to take it to the *D'rhissh* city in the sands."

If he had said, "It's a poison spider and I want you to put it down your blouse," I would have had a better reaction to it. Psiboxes were dangerous, illegal. They got inside your mind, into your feelings. They did stuff to you, weird stuff. They were the ultimate drug, the ultimate power, the ultimate destruction. They ate your mind, they warped your personality, they made you . . . do things.

I shook my head. "I don't think so," I said.

He looked at me with those Bethdish eyes and I felt the melting again. "C'mon," he pleaded softly, "it would mean so much to me. I could pay you handsomely. I could get you your licenses, your ship back, everything. I could do a lot for you, more than we can talk about here."

I looked at the thing and it looked harmless enough. It sat there on that hairy, long-fingered hand, and I felt his other hand squeeze my jumpsuited thigh gently, persuasively. Images swarmed through my imagination like warm liquid.

No one's ever accused me of having anything of steel, including resolve, determination or thighs. "Okay," I breathed, still locked into his eyes. "I'll do it. I'll do it now."

He smiled and I felt a grin on my own face. At that moment, I would have done anything he asked, anything.

He put the little box on the counter and signaled to Trixie who brought us another round of frin juice. "To success," he toasted, his other hand still squeezing gently, rhythmically. I gulped the juice.

It was almost seven-thirty in the morning and I was considering an encounter with a homely Bethdish Stellar Confiscation Officer who just offered me one of the creepiest smuggling jobs I ever saw. "Hey, N'Doro," I called out, "wait for me here."

Two days later N'Doro was in the co-pilot's seat and I was wearing the captain's headset and maneuvering the *Linda Rae* above the shimmering sands of Bethdish's toxic deserts to the coordinates we had been given. Stellar Confiscation Officer Kraygg was a fond memory, which occasionally caused me to smile or even grin, and the psibox was safely stowed in the secret cargo compartment under my seat. We even had a few spare credits to shop with, and it looked like the psibox thing was going to be a piece of cake.

I was grinning at the controls and deciding what I would buy on the next Toshiba run when I got that prickly feeling in the back of my neck that says something is very wrong, extremely wrong, wronger than you can possibly know.

N'Doro looked over at me and I saw beads of sweat gleaming on his ebony face. "Captain," he whispered, "I feel funny..."

The ship made a sharp nosedive toward the ground and it took all my concentration to pull her up into a glide path on a slow descent. We were still about thirty klicks from the spot where Kraygg wanted us to toss out the box.

N'Doro slumped back in his seat and I could see that he had lost consciousness. I took over his controls as well as my own and hoped our filtration systems were go as we bumped into the poisoned atmosphere of the *D'rhissh* desert.

You know, they always say any landing you walk away from is a good one, but they don't ever take Bethdish into consideration, do they?

I looked out of the little control window and all I could see was the middle of a sandstorm. I knew the temperature out there was something that wouldn't support humanoid life forms, and the swirling air was a mix of poison and *D'rhissh* viruses, the stuff that supported the scorpion-like creatures. They were not only sentient, they were damned intelligent, the diplomats of the universe, but they did live in an area that was strictly off-limits to everyone else.

I knew the minute Kraygg gave me the coordinates that he wanted me to drop the box into *D'rhissh* territory. I had no idea what the thing would do to the *D'rhissh*, maybe disrupt them completely, start a war or something. And I knew that such a thing was forbidden. I knew it, but it didn't matter. At the time, it didn't matter. Nothing but Kraygg mattered.

However, after a crash into the *D'rhissh* compound thirty klicks from the Sacred City, I was having second thoughts. You ever see a big scorpion? I mean one six feet tall with sharp legs and a whiplike tail with a stinger the size of your nightmares on it? You ever see an armed contingent of them coming toward your beat-up spacecraft? I thought not.

I glanced at N'Doro's peaceful face and was thankful that he would be spared the horror. I genuinely liked my handsome, less-than-swift co-pilot. I was gonna miss him. Hell, it looked like I was soon gonna miss everything.

The scraping and clanging at the hatch was insistent, and I knew that a breach would cause me to breathe the air and the *D'rhissh* viruses and that would be that. I would be choked on a soufflé of expanding viral tendrils in my nose, throat, everywhere. I guess I did the heroic thing and passed out myself.

"Welcome," the thing said, its translator box giving it a distinguished and cultured sound. It wore the ribbon sash of an interstellar ambassador and its tail sprang back and forth. The claws were drawn in as far as possible.

I was lying on a divan covered in purple silk in a great hall. A tube up my nose fed me oxygen, and my other nostril was sealed. I looked around. The ceiling was exquisite, coffered in black and gold and the walls were hung with swaths of draperies. N'Doro was snoring loudly through his tube on another divan, and on yet a third, a giant scorpion lay on its stomach, its legs falling over the sides and its strange insectoid face looking at me, first with one eye, then another. The reclining *D'rhissh* was decorated with small flashing jewels on its head and thorax.

"Welcome," the upright one repeated, "and thank you for delivering the psibox. I am Krizhhisk-ak. We were afraid Kraygg-rhieashh would not be able to find anyone to do it. We applaud your courage, Cookie Sullivan-rhieashh, progenitor of our house." The thing used the formal suffix reserved for royalty, heads of state and one's mother. I wasn't technically related to any of the *D'rhissh*, although there had been, well, A Past Incident, which rendered me a ceremonial sort of *D'rhissh* mother or father or something. I swear, I never touched the scorpion in question, but their mating habits, well, it's a whole other story.

"Huh?" I said in my usual fit of eloquence.

"Honored guest," the reclining *D'rhissh* spoke in a soft voice, "accept our deepest thanks. We know how the humanoid races have tried to keep the psiboxes to themselves, to the detriment of interstellar peace. The power of the box is very great over humanoids, but as you may know, it has no such power over us." Its tail made a switching motion and I saw that the stinger tip was also bejeweled. "With another box safe in our keeping, the treaty discussions may move forward without interference to the humanoid delegates."

I tried to digest this bit of news. Wouldn't you know it, the boxes only worked on people. Who woulda thought?

The sashed *D'rhissh* with the cultured voice box paced rapidly back and forth, agitated. "My Queen," he said in his own language, which sounded something like a cross between a cricket chirping and a wooden barrel breaking up, "we must assure the visitors, especially the esteemed Pilot-rhieashh."

"Yes, yes," the Queen said impatiently. "I am sure they have figured it out. You never give them credit for intelligence, the way I do." It turned an eye to me. "My honored Father wishes me to assure you that the *D'rhissh* virus will not harm you. We administered an inoculant as soon as the Imperial Guard hatched you from your conveyance. And the air you are absorbing is the same as your usual mix."

Oh, good. I hadn't even given it a thought, figuring we would just die a hero's death. Well, a *D'rhissh* hero's death.

I was treated to more nice words, then I expressed a wish to go home. The prospect of a scorpion banquet or whatever other honors they had in mind didn't really thrill me, but I tried to be as nice as I knew how, especially as I was sort of related to about two hundred of them.

N'Doro didn't wake up until we were back on the *Linda Rae*. The *D'rhissh* had fumigated the ship and even tidied up a bit. He didn't know that we had done a good thing, and I decided to let his conscience rest rather than overburdening it with that kind of information.

But I couldn't help thinking about Kraygg. What was in this for him? It was dangerous for him to intercept psiboxes - the kind of people who traded in that stuff were dirty, dangerous, and unpredictable. Well, more so than me and N'Doro, I mean. And for him to risk everything by sending them to the *D'rhissh*. He could lose his job and everything. I didn't get it.

I didn't get it until later that night, in the Mare Inebrium where I had gone to celebrate the return of my ship, my career, and my life, not to mention the psibox, which I wisely didn't mention. I was sitting at the bar as Trixie kept the Zombie Cocktails coming, picking and choosing which space rat or offworld pile of neurons and gasoline I was going to accept drinks from.

I thought about Kraygg, and how for someone not all that attractive - repulsive, in fact - I sure had found him irresistible for a couple of days. Suddenly I knew exactly why he was in the psibox game as dangerous as it was. I sighed. It was a long way to go, but it's true - some guys will do anything for a date.

ROOTS

Cultivating diplomatic relations can be difficult

I hate it when I have to learn something the hard way. This implies that there might have been an easier way to learn something, but that's not always true. Sometimes the hard way is the only way, and you end up starting a war or something over it.

Like a few years ago, when I was still on the shuttle run between Mare Tranq and Otherside, our two big lunar bases, piloting a bucket of bolts and duct tape on an expired transport license. My sometimes-co-pilot, N'Doro, had taken a vacation and was languishing amid the splendors of three square meals a day and all the exercise you could hope for in the penal camp at Mare Nec. I forget exactly which brawl that little stay at the Corporation's expense was about, but maybe it was the one in which my six-foot companion punched the living daylights out of a Corporation VIP, having mistaken him for a "ferret-faced piece of offworld effluvium," whatever the hell that was.

Anyway, I was on my own, transporting miners back and forth between the mines at Otherside and the pleasure palaces at Mare Tranq. Both bases had large ports and were fully equipped for real space travel, but Mare Tranq was the only one that qualified as an actual city rather than just an overblown Corporation settlement. The work was dull and monotonous, but the occasional bit of creative transportation, read smuggling, made it worth the effort.

The trip from Otherside to Mare Tranq was usually a raucous affair, with a dozen or so miners wanting to part with their paychecks. I charged exorbitantly for the liquor and let them get all worked up before I dropped them at the door to one of the shadier sex parlors. The owners, Lester and Big Red Snipely, gave me a small kickback.

The trip back was always very quiet, with a dozen or so miners badly hung over and trying not to puke or even move.

There wasn't a big call for smuggling - just the usual stuff the Corporation wouldn't let the miners have back at Otherside. I hauled in cigarettes, dope, offworld booze and once in a while a young lady or boy or something, always with their consent, of course. I even smuggled in someone's mother once, for crying out loud, but that nearly got me into a lot of trouble. Usually it was just enough to break the routine and give me pocket money.

But this trip, Lester and Big Red had something for me.

"Just take this to Otherside," Big Red said, in her working uniform of two wisps of red lace and a cork. She handed me a small pet carrier, the kind with breathing holes and a little metal gate through which something that looked like a wise old turnip stared me down with luminous brown eyes.

"What is it?" I asked. I had seen quite a few interesting things, but a sentient root vegetable was a first.

"A customer left it here," she said. "I dunno what it is, some kind of Martian ground digger or something. Anyway, here's the address." She handed me a slip of paper with an Otherside mining barracks number on it.

"Okay," I said, slinging the carrier over my shoulder. "Usual rates, though." What was I thinking?

I picked up the miners - there were eleven of them, looking like Death - and put the kitty carrier in N'Doro's co-pilot chair next to mine in the scarred and peeling anteway we grandly called "The Bridge." I guided the *Linda Rae* through a queasy take-off then went to the passenger compartment to make sure all eleven survived whether they felt like it or not. They looked like they were waiting for rigor mortis to either set in or wear off, so I went back to the bridge with a cup of synthetic tea and the latest copy of 'Shuttle Digest.'

I was halfway through an article about avoiding the speed traps near Mars Colony, not that my crate would have made Mars Colony, much less been noticed in a speed trap, in a lunar month.

"Excuse me," a disembodied voice piped up, "but I need to get out and walk around a bit."

"Sorry, pal," I said without looking up. "Once we take off, we can't open the door. No air out there, you know. Just go back and sit down and we'll be landing real soon."

I got 'em once in a while - the after effects of lunar liquor could be pretty devastating. I even had one guy actually try to open the door and walk out. We were cruising at about two thousand meters over the desolate and rocky surface. I was tempted, let me tell you, but I just talked him into going back to his seat quietly.

"No," the voice said patiently, too patiently for a miner, "I want to get out of the cage."

I felt a little prickle on the back of my neck. It was the turnip. It was talking.

"Uh, where do you want to go?" I asked. I was sure the sight of a walking and talking turnip would upset the miners. So far, no one had thrown up this time out. I sorta wanted to keep it that way.

"Just let me out for a few minutes," it said. "I am cramped in here."

I picked up the cage and looked through the gate. The thing seemed harmless enough.

"Okay," I said to it, "but you'll have to stay here on the bridge. I don't want you frightening the passengers." I opened the cage door and watched as the turnip-headed thing crawled out. It had little arms and legs which seemed to lengthen and contract as necessary. It climbed down from the chair and paced around on the floor. It couldn't have been more than half a meter high, even with its legs stretched out to the maximum.

"So," I said by way of conversation, "what are you?" I could see the smooth creamy flesh of its head, turning to a sort of lavender then purple at the edges. That was what really gave it the appearance of a turnip I decided. The arms and legs projected directly out from the head and there was a flat blade-like structure in the back like a rudder. It had a faintly aquatic look about it. A water turnip.

The face had no expression. The eyes, large and luminous, were the main feature, but there was a tiny mouth almost hidden underneath them. There was no nose.

"I am what your kind calls a Martian digger, as your friend in Mare Tranq rightly guessed." Its voice was soft and well-modulated, with a tiny bit of a patrician accent, as though it had learned its Chinglish in a formal school.

"Wow, I thought you guys were a myth," I said admiringly. "So how come you're in a cage bound for Otherside?" The Martian diggers were rare, a life form too intelligent to have much truck with the dregs of the human race. When we first colonized Mars, they made themselves known, then all but disappeared. As a First Contact, it was spectacularly disappointing, probably to both sides.

I guessed they just sort of disappeared into legend or wherever else things that have seen and dismissed the human race went. It was probably getting crowded there, but what did I know?

"I am actually a diplomatic envoy," the turnip said. "I have agreed to this mode of transportation for security reasons." It was on the floor flexing its legs in some sort of rhythmic motion, root cellar aerobics, maybe.

"Security reasons," I said. "Then why are you telling me? Wait a minute. I picked you up in a kitty cage at a brothel for crying out loud." I knew the turnip was lying.

It stopped exercising and climbed back up to the cage. "Okay," it admitted. "I'm not a diplomatic envoy. I'm a spy."

"Well, that's more like it," I said. I mean, that I could believe. James Bond from the vegetable garden.

It settled back into the bit of towel on which it had reclined in the cage. The gate was open and its little feet dangled out. "We have several hours," it estimated correctly. "I will tell you the story. Then I will have to kill you." Its large eyes blinked seriously

"Yeah, just tell me the story, pal," I said. "You'll probably kill me with boredom." Or food poisoning, I thought.

"In the beginning," he began, and I braced myself for a long two hours, "we slumbered beneath the rocks and sand as the red winds blew unnoticed far above us and we were immobile. The security of our world was all around us, pressing in on every side in safety. We communicated through this sleeptime with our thoughts, and for time immeasurable, we stayed in silent stillness."

I flipped on my recorder. It occurred to me that a Martian digger's story might be of some value.

"Then the noises came. Far above us, on the surface where we had never ventured, there was noise. We ignored this as it was happening in a part of the world which we did not inhabit, the useless surface world. But it did not go away. It was a long time between the beginning of the noise and the great disaster which your kind wrought upon us, but in those days time meant nothing to us. We had no regular motions of the planets to track, no sun, no stars. We had only the interior life.

"When the first burrows were breached and our people were dug out of their homes and heaped up like so much refuse, we tried to protest. But we had been silent for so long that we had no voice. It took more time for us to develop a way to speak. By then, hundreds of thousands of us had been excavated and killed in great rotting heaps."

This wasn't the way I had heard it, but I had heard it from the other side, from a construction worker. The guy who told me about it just shook his head. "Yeah," he admitted, "we dug 'em up. We thought they were food. But they were tough and stringy and tasted like shit, so we threw 'em away. We were diggin' around there to put in the foundations for the landing site. We didn't know they were intelligent. Hell, we thought they were potatoes or something."

An easy mistake, I thought, looking at the creature's head again. The few tiny sprouts of fibrous hairs on its wrinkly pate resembled the micro-roots which are always so hard to clean on regular vegetables, the ones you try to scrub off with a stiff brush.

The Martian continued. "And then we found our voices and tried again to communicate, but it did no good. And we found our legs and arms and our steering blades and with mobility we were able to flee. But our life underground and undisturbed was over."

"So, where'd you all go?" I asked. I was mesmerized by the critter. I had heard spooky tales of the early attempts to eat them, stories of soups, stews, and butter sauces which invariably ended in severe stomach cramps. It was the sort of story mothers told children to get them to stop putting dirty things into their mouths. Well, my mother, anyway.

"We went into the mountains where there was nothing to attract your kind," it answered. "Those of us who were left," it added.

There was a short silence before it continued.

"But we had learned our bitter lessons. We adapted to life above the ground and studied your kind. We abandoned our sedentary ways and became physically active, developing our arms and legs into the useful appendages you see now. And we kept thinking and planning and absorbing all we could."

It eyed me with the faintest suggestion of smugness. "And now we are ready," it said.

"Oh, yeah?" I said. "Ready for what?" What were they going to do, I wondered. Rise up in their tiny crock-pots and wage war on us?

"We have a business proposition for you," it replied. "We have knowledge of the interiors of planets. We are superbly suited to underground operations of all sorts. And we control more than half of the Martian surface."

"So how come you're hitching a ride to Otherside?" I queried. "What's so interesting there?"

The critter rolled its luminous eyes. Talking to me must have been sorta like talking to a dog, I guess.

"The mines. You are mining minerals at Otherside and I need to see your mining operations. No one would let me see anything in my present form, but masquerading as someone's pet is a perfect disguise. My miner will take me everywhere and I will see everything."

"Yeah," I said, "so what? So you see everything, big deal. There's nothing secret there anyway." Well, there might have been, but I was hardly in a position to know that sort of stuff.

The critter spoke to me patiently, the way you might explain something to a three-year-old.

"Your world depends on the resources you find in other places. Your world no longer supports you - the mines at Otherside supply more than half the requirements of your home planet. What would happen if that resource dried up?"

"We'd be up the creek with no paddle," I admitted. "But how're a couple of guys like you gonna take over the largest corporate entities in the universe?"

"Oh, that part is easy," he said. "The hard part is running things once we have them. That's why we need you, why we can't just destroy the human race outright."

Well, that was a relief. No sudden obliteration of the human race by vegetables. Whew. Had me worried there for a moment.

"So we can stick around as partners, is that it?" I asked.

"Well, in a very general sense," the digger said.

Okay, the human race subordinated to a race of roots. Well, it beat extinction, I guess.

Let me state right here for the record, that it never once occurred to me that the little critter might be a danger to the human race or even just myself. If I had thought any danger whatsoever existed, I would have planted his shriveled little rump in about eight meters of rocky lunar dust and left him. But come on. He looked totally harmless.

As we neared Otherside, the creature grew silent and crept all the way back up into the kitty carrier. I reached over and strapped it in for landing, dragging N'Doro's seat belt across it.

The landing was okay, everyone survived, and no miners threw up until they had cleared the shuttle. That's what I call a successful trip.

I checked on the thing - it hadn't given me a name and when I inquired, it seemed to be at a loss for words. "We don't do that," it finally replied.

You'd think if something had delusions of conquering the known universe, it would at least have a name for itself. But it seemed okay, so I unhooked the safety belt and slung the carrier over my shoulder. I rechecked the address Big Red had given me and started out toward the mining residence elevators.

Mining operations, to include residences and everything else, were all under the lunar surface. Back when we first colonized the moon, there was a lot of environmental concern over the lunar surface, and it had been forbidden to disturb it, except at Mare Tranq, which on romantic moonlight nights on Earth resembled a bulbous scab.

I located the host miner, a guy named Bertie Huggins, turned over my cargo, collected a nice little fee, and went back to my shuttle.

That should have been the end of it, right?

Wrong.

Three days and a trip to Mare Tranq later and I'm looking at the furrowed face of one of the toughest magistrates on the lunar surface, namely Hizzoner Judge Malcolm Conley, or 'Malcontent' as he was known in legal and other circles.

"Where's the alien life form?" he bellowed at me, ceremonial gavel raised dangerously close to my head.

"If you mean the turnip in the pet carrier," I said, "I delivered it to one Bertie Huggins at Barracks 4, Otherside Mines." I had on my best "who, me?" expression.

The judge didn't buy it. "Smuggling," he said with a twisted little smile, "willful disregard for offworld quarantine laws, transporting live cargo without a permit, operating a shuttle on an expired license, and causing a public disturbance!" He grinned triumphantly.

I was puzzled. Why would the worst judge in Mare Tranq be picking on me? Okay, so I was guilty of most of that stuff, but no one ever enforced those laws. What was going on?

A weasel-guy in the uniform of a Corporation inspector addressed the court. "Your Honor," he said with more than a trace of self-important arrogance in his voice, "we are aware of these heinous crimes. However, the Corporation will choose to overlook them if Ms. Sullivan surrenders the alien life form." The Corporation could choose to overlook anything it liked - it had no jurisdiction on Mare Tranq.

And besides, Ms. Sullivan, namely me, didn't have the damned life form. The life form was delivered to a miner. I pointed this out to the Corporation inspector and Hizzoner.

Malcontent banged his gavel again, reminding me of the traffic judge in Mr. Toad's Wild Ride. "Guilty!" he shouted. "Guilty, guilty, guilty!" He grinned and I remembered the rumors about happy drugs.

The Corporation weasel rolled his eyes and waited patiently before continuing in the same arrogant little whine. "In that case, Your Honor, we will give Ms. Sullivan exactly forty-eight hours to either produce the life form or be taken into custody." Considering they didn't have any jurisdiction, they sure had a lot of pull.

Malcontent grinned again and banged the gavel a few more times. The bailiff escorted me out of the courtroom, removed his earplugs, and returned my personal possessions, which had been confiscated. "Go," he said curtly with the eloquence of a man unused to speaking aloud.

I went.

Forty-eight hours isn't very long when you have been given some impossible task. I left my co-pilot N'Doro in the slammer in Mare Nec where he was still sleeping it off and went back to Otherside, this time without any paying passengers, a situation which pained me.

I politely knocked on Bertie Huggins' door and waited for him to open it. I waited with my Glock Stingray set on "stun - maybe kill."

Bertie did not open the door, however. The force of my polite knocking caused the door to fall inward and reveal a gaping pit where the floor had presumably been. Bertie, having outlived his usefulness, was propped lifeless on the remains of the kitchen counter, a dreamy look on his expired face and a dead hand caressing the upturned kitty carrier. He hadn't been dead too long from the looks of him.

I looked down into the pit. It went down forever, past half a mile of living quarters, administrative offices, stores, amusements, equipment, and all the other usual detritus of a lunar mining operation. It was sorta neat, like an exploded diagram or something.

I sighed. The damned turnip was going to be a lot more trouble than I thought.

It was at this point that I could have informed the Corporation of my suspicions and left the search up to them. I guess I would have suffered the consequences and gone to jail in Mare Tranq for my accumulated tickets, but at least humanity might have had a chance of escaping war and enslavement. I don't know. At any rate, I made the other decision, the wrong one. I started looking for the devil turnip myself.

The breach in Mr. Huggins' quarters, not to mention the hole in that entire portion of the Corporation's valuable resources, caused alarms to go off and security officers to respond. I was peering into the hole and wondering how I could get down it when a security cruiser came screaming up at full siren and I did what any reasonable person would do. I jumped.

I'm no hero - I was going to jump down it anyway. Lunar surface, remember? One-sixth gravity. I didn't exactly float, but when I came to a halt at the bottom, I was okay, just a little bruised up from hitting various bits of junk sticking out on the way down.

A crude tunnel loomed before me and I had no time for fancy thought-processes. I scurried down it like a rat.

I reached the light at the end of the tunnel and realized that I was too late. The mines were deserted, devoid of any human occupants. I ran wildly from machine to machine, looking in every command post, every security cubicle, every office. Nothing, or rather, no one.

I sat down on the cold dirt floor and thought about crying. There didn't seem to be any point to it, though, so I just waited for the Corporation security guys to fly by and pick me up. Somehow, jail at Mare Tranq no longer seemed to so bad.

But they never did. Everyone knows what happened after that, how once the turnips had a foothold, so to speak, in the lunar mines, it was an easy transition to overthrowing the Corporation. The diggers established themselves as the dominant species on Mars and the moon, and probably would have gone for Old Earth itself if it weren't for the water.

The water, you see, is what finally kept them from conquering the earth, although since we have no resources on the earth, we have to buy them at exorbitant rates from the diggers. They can't stand the water. They developed without water and were very susceptible to mold, mildew, and just plain drowning. But it took us awhile to figure this out, and in the meantime, we lost the Martian and lunar colonies and were confined to the earth in a sort of economic subjugation, supplying slave labor to the mines in exchange for basic raw materials.

I got out of the lunar mines by laboriously climbing up the hole and evading the diggers. I knew what to look for, the spindly legs, the rudder, the fleshy purple-tinged head. I made it to the *Linda Rae*, and then to Mare Nec where I stopped just long enough to pick up the still-comatose form of my partner from the city jail and fly to Old Earth before the war started. In the pre-war confusion, no one seemed to notice me.

The war dragged on for a couple of years and ended in the usual way, with a lot of complicated trade agreements and sanctions and tariffs and things. N'Doro and I made a pretty fair living during the war, hauling supplies and stuff, but if we had really been on the ball, we would have gone into turnip farming. The Army used millions of 'em as decoys.

My part in starting the Martian wars never came out, and as far as I know, I never saw the original digger from the kitty carrier again. But I worked in the Resistance - we didn't call it the Underground for obvious reasons - and hoped that my efforts there might alleviate some of the guilt I felt over the whole thing.

Some day maybe the human race will rise up again to conquer the stars, this time watching out for what's under its feet.

The Tanneh Death Chop

A Mare Inebrium Story by Kate Thornton

Mare Inebrium Universe created by Dan Hollifield

There's never really an end to a story - I mean, in real life episodes come and go, but there's always more. Even when someone dies, the story goes on. But life is full of starts, isn't it? Remember that when you finish this story.

The day it all started for me - don't ask me why I call it a "day" when everyone knows there's no such thing as night or day on a junk cargo shuttle in cold space - anyway, when it began I was on my way to Toshiba Station in Mare Nec Sector, just a quick run to Otherside from Mare Tranq. It was a lunar smuggling job, not to put too fine a point on it.

My ship, the *Linda Rae*, was not suitable for extended interplanetary travel, mostly on account of being an old converted passenger shuttle which had, through the years of neglect, been converting itself to a pile of rusting bolts, duct tape and spit.

The *Linda Rae* was half of my father's generous legacy to me, the other half being the ability to fly anything that could lift off a surface. Oh, and he taught me most of my smuggling skills, too, may he rest in peace. I know he probably wanted a boy, but one of the other things he taught me was that you make the best of what you've got. "Play the hand you're dealt, Cookie," he used to say, "and make sure you win."

Of course, I don't run the *Linda Rae* all by myself. I have a big handsome co-pilot, N'Doro, who makes up for his dim wits with a beautiful smile and a body that can make grown women - and some men - weep. He's the perfect partner in my commercial endeavors, although when he makes me weep, it's usually just from exasperation. Okay, maybe I do run the craft all by myself.

Anyway, N'Doro was snoring softly in the co-pilot's seat as I maneuvered the *Linda Rae* across the moon's rocky terrain, flying low and slow to avoid drawing any unwanted attention from the local authorities. I kept her steady, mindful of the carefully packed shipment of contraband chocolates in the secret cargo compartment under my seat. I didn't want to jostle them around too much as they were filled with a mixture of chocolate cream and krik, a high explosive drug that was all the rage in the lunar mining settlements.

The gauges on my console were all reading "optimum" and for a second I imagined what it would be like if everything on board really did work. Then I snapped back to reality as a shock wave hit the craft and I regretted intensely that I had been foolish enough to pack explosive chocolates right under my butt. Even a social life as dead as mine doesn't deserve that kind of a boost.

N'Doro's beautiful ebony features were still and relaxed as a second shock wave sent us spinning toward a big pile of dead rocks. N'Doro could sleep through anything. I wrestled with the steering mechanism and the *Linda Rae* responded with all the grace and enthusiasm of a sullen teenager, pouting and bucking as I managed to avoid a fatal collision with the lunar surface.

It wasn't until we were even lower and slower than I thought possible that I realized the cargo had not accidentally discharged. I looked at the ancient computer screen and read it twice to make sure. The cargo had not exploded. We had been fired upon and hit.

"Hey, N'Doro!" I screamed, "Wake up! Someone's shooting at us!"

His lovely dark eyes fluttered open and a look of incomprehension slowly crossed his lovely face. It crossed so slowly that it was still there when I threw him a weapon from my side locker. His reflexes were superb and he caught the Glock Stingray before he was even aware of waking up.

"Huh?"

"I said, someone's shooting at us. Take this and go have a look."

He swung gracefully to his feet, set the Glock on "kill" and made for the aft screens. Only one of the exterior sensors was working and it just registered the dead surface of the moon.

"Don't see nuthin' Captain," N'Doro called.

"Check for leaks," I shouted back. Minor leaks on the hull were self-sealing, but the glop always leaked through and smelled like the inside of an old pressure suit. Just the thought of that smell made me gag.

"Nope," N'Doro shouted, "Don't see nuthin'. You sure somethin' happened? I didn't feel nuthin."

I sighed. If we had been blown to smithereens, N'Doro wouldn't have felt anything. Well, okay, I guess I wouldn't have either. But I knew what I had seen on the screen. I printed the sensor audit. There. There it was. Two projectiles the size of a standard credit had hit the hull of the *Linda Rae*. They hadn't pierced the tough outer shell, but they had been flung with enough velocity to register on the nearly non-functional sensor, the velocity of a weapon.

By the time I worked this out, the lights of Toshiba Station illuminated the horizon and I went into landing mode. We were carrying a legit cargo of sex discs and junk food for the Corporation store, so we landed over on the commercial port and waited for the inspectors to come by for bribes. N'Doro usually handled that part of things. He busied himself in the bribe locker, choosing carefully. Toshiban inspectors usually wanted either new sex discs or real liquor and we gave this one both.

"You guys got a couple of sore spots on your hull," he observed as he stashed the loot in his bribe bag. "You tick anybody off out there?"

I shook my head and N'Doro just grinned.

"See you around," the inspector said as he pencil whipped our docking report and left without so much as a glance toward the built-up area under the Captain's chair, my chair.

N'Doro saw to the maintenance and I did the post-flight checks before we stepped out of the stale recirc of the *Linda Rae* and into the stale recirc of Toshiba Station. I gave N'Doro a twenty-four hour pass and watched him disappear toward the Corporation gambling houses. I sighed again. At least he didn't have too much to lose. I always paid him after we left a Corporation outpost.

After the mech bots off loaded our legit cargo, I went in and packed up the good stuff into a soft padded bag. I planned to transport it to the usual place, same as always, where I would pick up my payment and head over to a pleasure palace for a few hours steam massage and holographic fantasy. I was already humming a nameless little tune as I slung the bag over my shoulder and gave my beloved wreck a fond backward look. My eyes widened.

I dropped the bag in surprise, then jumped out of the way as I remembered what was in it. I waited for the explosion. It didn't come - I must have packed that stuff very carefully indeed.

Only something really unusual would cause me to drop a bag full of chocolate krik.

On the hull of my ship, between the unmistakable little dents, smoke or fire or something had made another mark, a mark far more disturbing to me than the dings of a light antipersonnel weapon. Etched in the steel hull of my shuttle craft was the black mark of a Tanneh chop.

Now, there are a few scary things in the universe, not the least of which is my taste in men, but that Tanneh chop was in a completely different league.

To start with, Tanneh was a long way from the Mare Nectaris sector of the Earth's moon. It was technically out of my reach, as the *Linda Rae* was okay as far as, say, the mining colonies on Mars maybe. But interstellar stuff was way out of my ballpark.

Also, Tanneh was a forbidden place. Although the whole place was shrouded in fear, no one seemed to know exactly why, and that made it all the scarier. I had heard it was off limits because the atmosphere was deadly poison, the natives were extremely hostile and there were no exploitable elements to hold the Corporation's interest. Of course, these conditions had never stopped the human race before, so there had to be something else, something really creepy.

I had also heard that Tanneh inhabitants were not even vaguely humanoid, but rather ethnocentric and given to meting out instant death to traders, explorers and members of the scientific community.

They were rumored to have some elaborate social system involving tribes or something and each tribe or clan had its own signature or chop. These chops, it was said, were used to claim territory and announce imminent destruction. I had seen a few of them sketched on a dock bulletin once and I knew one when I saw one. And I was looking at one on the underbelly of my ship.

I peered more closely at the dents and wondered about the weapon used. If the intention had been to destroy my ship, which was in the slow process of destroying itself anyway, the regular little pockmarks on the hull were pitiful. But if someone had fired upon the *Linda Rae* merely to set a Tanneh death chop, then I was in very big trouble.

And worse, I didn't know why.

And why hadn't the Toshiban port inspector mentioned the Tanneh death chop? Okay, port inspectors were trained to close their eyes and stick out their hands, but you'd think something like that would at least rate a mention.

I was worried about leaving my death-marked ship in a public dock where a Tanneh force bomb might take out half the populated sector and earn me a personal place in local history.

But there wasn't much I could do about it, so I picked up my cargo of chocolate liqueur creams in the padded bag which I had thoughtfully labeled, "human organ donations" and caught the roller from Toshiba docks to the Inebrium.

The Inebe, as everyone called it, was the retirement brainchild of an old friend of mine. Dan Holly modeled his Toshiban bar after the one on Bethdish. You really have to wonder about someone whose lifelong ambition and childhood dream involved a bar, but Dan was a good guy in lots of ways and the Inebe was like a second home to me. Okay, not having a real home made the Inebe my first home, but I am too delicate and sensitive to ever admit that.

Anyway, the krik chocolates were for Dan and as soon as I got there, I set the "human organ donations" on the table next to the previous customer's nearly-empty glass and flung myself into a booth.

"Hey, Beautiful!" a cheery, if somewhat metallic, voice ground out.

Dan Holly had flown with my Daddy in his youth. That was back when the moon was the only exploitable off-Earth entity and first contact was just a science fiction dream. He had gone on to pilot the big Corporation starships – heck, we even served on a starship together in your youth, but an accident with a Corporation hovercraft had left him with a pair of plastic legs and a metallic edge to his voice.

The intervening years could have provided Dan with regenerated limbs made from his own genetic material and a voice as sweet as an Irish tenor's, but he refused.

"I'm used to myself like this," he claimed. But I think that in a world where even the most comprehensive medical problems could be fixed routinely, Dan liked being different.

I guess I liked it, too. The Corporation rewarded conformity, so those of us who didn't fit in too well were forced to live on the economic edge, the border between a boring and modestly successful existence and an interesting but unpredictable life. Dan and I had both chosen the latter, although I made my choice earlier than he made his.

Dan gave me an avuncular kiss and slid into the seat across from me. A roboserver brought me drink.

"So, Cookie," Dan said, "What's the haps?" His eyes shone in anticipation as he gazed fondly at me and at the pressure case on the table.

I reached over and snapped the locks on the case open. Dan lifted the hinged lid and swirling tendrils of mist fingered out over the edge of the box. Six dozen chocolates rested in their gold embossed ballotin on a bed of dry ice, just like they used to ship them in the old days. The big difference, of course, was each chocolate had been injected with a generous slug of krik.

Dan closed his eyes but kept on smiling, and placed a gold credit onto the table. "Oh, you've done it again," he said with a touch of dramatic reverence in his edgy voice.

I laughed. "Just don't eat them all at once," I said, slipping the single gold credit into a zip pocket on my jumpsuit. That single credit was worth about ten thousand ordinary credits, and it was more money than I had ever had at one time.

"You done good, Cookie," Dan said as the roboserver took the box of chocolates off the table and trundled away with it.

I knew my little job, dangerous as it was, wasn't going to feed hungry children or further galactic peace. But Dan's approval meant worlds to me, more than he knew. Like I said, the Inebe was a home to me and Dan was sorta like a father, only not in all ways, mind you, and we had done quite a few things that were very taboo in even the most liberal of family relationships.

I had fond memories of those times and let me tell you, plastic legs never got in my way, and that metallic voice can still make me all warm and breathless. Dan the man was definitely human in all the right places, not the least of which was his generous heart and his quick mind.

I didn't ask who the chocolates were for or what the profits - large profits - would go to, but I knew Dan. I knew, for example, that he didn't take many mind or body altering substances and anyway he was allergic to chocolate. The cargo was not for his personal use.

"So, Cooks," Don had called me that ever since he had first met me, and I had been in diapers at the time, "what's your plan?"

He waited patiently as I sipped my Zombie cocktail and got my thoughts together. I wanted to tell him about the Tanneh death chop on the *Linda Rae* but I didn't want to put him in any danger.

"It's okay," he said, "whatever it is, it can't hurt me." Dan had lived through a lot and was one tough guy, but he was still my best friend. On the other hand, I knew he would never forgive me if I kept something like that from him, so I told him everything.

Dan listened as I went through the whole story, starting with my cargo pickups at Mare Tranq and ending up in the Inebe.

"And the port inspector didn't mention the chop?" he asked.

I shook my head.

"Then he either didn't see it, in which case he had his eyes closed, or maybe he didn't want to see it, in which case he's been paid not to see it."

"Why?" I asked. "Who'd want the inspector bought off?" I couldn't believe the guy hadn't noticed a thirty-foot mark right between the two little dents he had taken such pains to point out.

Dan frowned and stared at the table. "Jeeze, Cooks, I think this whole thing is maybe my fault."

"Your fault?" I said incredulously. "How do you figure that?"

Dan sighed. "I shoulda told you all this a long time ago. Damn, we shoulda never got you in this all. But I guess I thought it would all turn out okay, you know?"

"No, I don't know, Dan," I said evenly. "Tell me what I'm in and how it could possibly be okay."

Dan sighed. He could tell I was curious, interested and about as pissed-off as the Zombie cocktail would permit.

"Okay, okay, it all really started before you were born, Cookie." I rolled my eyes. I don't care about the world before I was born, to be honest. And I hate those James-Michener-first-the-continents-were-formed stories, too.

"Your father and I were running cargo out of Harrison Schmidt to Sagan Colony, just a few runs on the side, you know? I had access to Corporation craft in those days and your dad had all the contacts, so we did a little business here and there."

I knew about that part of Dan's life. He and my father were best friends and it was the main reason why he became my best friend after Daddy went to that big cargo bay in the sky.

"Anyway," he continued, "we were running a little side job out to Sagan when this guy at Schmidt asks if we can take passengers. Now, getting from Schmidt to Sagan in those days was practically free, so this was a little weird. But he wanted passage with no questions asked, no Corporation paperwork, no nothing. Well, that was more or less our specialty - the no questions stuff - so he gave us a name and we took him to Sagan. A few days later, he wants to go to Mars Colony, same deal. After that, we saw him every few weeks, wanting a ride from one place to another, always using a different name and always paying up front and in cash. Over the next few months we musta taken that guy to every inhabited settlement in the system. He was nice, quiet, didn't cause any trouble and we sorta looked forward to taking him around."

Dan grinned. "Hey, the income was pretty good, and even when I couldn't get off from work, your Daddy would take him wherever he needed to go. We always had some kind of cargo to run, so life was pretty sweet. Heck, your Daddy bought a house for that nice girl who later became your Mamma, and me, well, I started savin' for this joint. We coulda spent the next twenty years taking this guy from place to place, but it didn't work out that way."

The grin faded. "One day he showed up - we were taking some ladies from New Chicago to Mare Tranq - and said he wanted us to take him to Tanneh."

Dan paused as the roboserver brought us each another drink. I wasn't thirsty, but something told me I was going to need it. I sipped at the rim of my Zombie slowly, gingerly. I knew where a fast slug of Zombie would take me, and I wasn't ready to go there yet.

"Well, we didn't do it. It was the first time we had ever had to tell the guy no, and he was pretty disappointed. We were afraid we might not see him again and we had grown used to all that extra money, but even then there were some things we just wouldn't do."

"But we changed our minds, Cooks. I got some time off work, borrowed the same old interplanetary I always used, and told the guy I'd take him. Your Daddy didn't really want any part of it, but you were on the way and he figured he could use the money, so in the end he agreed to go with us."

Dan stared hard into his empty glass. "I was scared, Cookie. I guess I just did things back then without thinking, things I'd be too scared to do now, and I don't know what made me go through with it. I guess I didn't have anything to lose. But your Daddy, he did it for you."

I shivered. Daddy was a brave and reckless guy alright, but Tanneh was way beyond brave or reckless or even foolish. Tanneh was death.

"So we took the guy to Tanneh. The trip was pretty easy, except for when we came across a Corporation cruiser halfway there and the captain wanted to chat. We shook the cruiser and continued on into Tanneh space, and I can tell you, when I saw that whirling globe of greenish gas, I broke out in a cold sweat.

"But your Daddy was pretty cheerful, playing decks-and-ladders with our passenger and cracking a few jokes. He beat him fair and square a coupla times, too. The passenger, who said his name was Frank that trip, seemed pretty calm, so I guess I was the only one sweating it out as we entered that green atmosphere."

Dan paused and I heard the rasp of his plastic legs as he shifted in his chair a little. "Tanneh's not what you think. I was nervous, but I sure wanted to see what it was like, and Frank told us not to worry, that he was expected and that no harm would come to us. And I believed him, I really did."

"Our communications went dead as we descended into the mists and I had no idea where we were going to land. Our power blinked off and the life-support systems came on, a little rusty but still serviceable, and the ship came to rest very gently and slowly in a large plaza. I swear your Daddy was praying or something."

"Frank opened the hatches and walked right out. He said the air was safe and I ran a check with the first aid kit before we followed him out. We were right in the middle of thousands of people, all of them smiling. They looked just like regular folks, Cookie, not a monster or anything among them."

"Frank introduced us to the head guys and we were escorted to some kind of a palace. They treated us well, Cooks," Dan said wistfully, "better than we'd been treated anywhere else. We had nice rooms, hot baths and a banquet and I wondered about all those horror stories we'd always been told. Frank seemed to be a pretty high-ranking guy and everyone else was real nice, too, only I noticed that no one talked much, and only Frank spoke to us. I thought at the time that maybe they just didn't know how to speak Chinglish or something."

"Anyway, the next day Frank told us we could go home and even paid us a nice little bonus. I was delighted to know we were going to get off Tanneh without any trouble, but I didn't count on your Daddy's sense of commerce."

"Your Daddy spent quite some time talking Frank's ears off, trying to negotiate some kind of a trading treaty or something. Frank just smiled and took us back to the plaza where our ship was."

"Instead of thousands of people milling around, there was just these three old guys waiting for us. They bowed to Frank and then they spent a bunch of time just looking at him. Then the old guys looked at each other and finally bowed to Frank again. Frank turned to us and smiled."

'We will agree to only one of your requests,' he said to your Daddy. 'There will be only one more safe trip back to Tanneh. You understand why we cannot trade with your worlds.'

"Well, maybe your Daddy understood, but I sure didn't. But somehow it wasn't the right time to ask about it, and I was glad just to get back on board my ship and watch Tanneh grow small in the viewer screen as we set our course for Mare Tranq."

"It was a long ride home, several days, so I asked your Daddy about the stuff he and Frank had talked about. He seemed pretty subdued, Cooks, and the story he told me made my stomach tighten up."

Dan waved to the roboserver and I was afraid he might get bombed on the Zombies and pass out before he finished the story, but he seemed stone cold sober. That alone was scary.

"To start with," he continued, "Frank wasn't just some important guy on Tanneh. He was the important guy, like the king or CEO or something. And he had been all over the inhabited system with us just to see what the place was like, especially all the places inhabited by the humanoid races. He was assessing us, Cooks, looking to see if we were worth saving or if we could all just be exterminated and leave Tanneh alone forever."

"You see, the Tanneh like their privacy - they like it a lot. They don't talk much because they're telepathic and this telepathy lets them hear everything any humanoid is thinking, and I mean everything. Cookie, Frank told your Daddy the first humanoid visitors to Tanneh scared them all spitless. They heard two conflicting things from each visitor, what they were saying and what they were thinking. And those early explorers and suchlike were thinking in terms of conquering and exploiting, concepts the Tanneh had never much developed. That's when the Tanneh planted some pretty gruesome horror stories in the survivors' minds and sent them back to scare off the rest of us."

They had done an excellent job, I thought. I was still scared of them.

"After long deliberation, the Tanneh Council of Elders decided to destroy the humanoid races, that it was way too risky to their own survival to allow them to exist. But Frank thought there must be some other way, some way in which minimal contact and the survival of the humanoid races could be maintained. He thought there might be a reason for human existence, maybe an evolutionary possibility down the road or something. He set out to gather information, and agreed with the Council of Elders that if he couldn't find any promising news, then the Tanneh would isolate themselves permanently from human contact. The easiest way for them to accomplish this would be total and permanent extermination of the humanoid races not native to Tanneh. We didn't know it at the time, but we had ferried Frank around from place to place on this quest, and had finally brought him home to make his decision."

I felt cold all over, and the Zombie cocktail in front of me seemed warm and friendly, even with the mist of melting ice over it. I was beyond shivering.

"When he told me all this, your Daddy was so quiet and serious that it scared me."

Quiet and serious was not exactly in his nature, as I knew quite well. I didn't know whether to believe Dan or laugh at this story, but his expression was grim.

"Frank had been thorough. As painful as it was for him to subject himself to the telepathic sludge of the known system, he went around looking for encouraging signs. We didn't know it at the time, of course, but Frank listened to everyone and everything, and he listened to your Daddy and me thinking more than anyone else."

"Daddy never mentioned any of this to me," I pointed out. "And we talked a lot, Dan. A lot." I kept the skepticism and a little edge of anger out of my voice. I guess I didn't want to believe that Daddy could have kept something that important from me. I mean, he told me everything.

Dan started talking again as though I hadn't said a word. "Frank and the elders decided to let the humanoid races live, just not anywhere near Tanneh. They kept up the stories about death to explorers and visitors and closed themselves off from further contact."

"Wouldn't it have been easier to just kill us all and live undisturbed?" I asked. I thought about how awful it would be to have to listen to everyone's innermost thoughts - disgusting, noisy, ceaseless.

Dan nodded. "Yeah, that's what I thought, too," he agreed. "But the Tanneh didn't see it that way. Good thing for us, I guess. Anyway, I wondered why they had just decided to leave us alone, but they didn't, really. You see, Frank made a deal with your Daddy."

I felt all queasy inside, like whatever Dan was going to say, I didn't want to hear any more. I tried to get up from the table, but I was paralyzed, probably from the Zombie.

"Cookie," Dan smiled, "Frank liked our thoughts. I know, I know, a coupla dumb shuttle rats, what's to like? But on all those flights with us, he listened in, and I guess he figured we were like, representative of our kind. I know I was usually thinking about work or something, but your Daddy was always thinking about you. Remember, you hadn't even been born yet, but he was, well, sorta obsessed with you."

That much I knew, thought he had been dead certain I would be a boy. Oh, well, some disappointments don't really matter, and once he had gotten over it, he never once treated me any different. I smiled at his memory.

"It was your Daddy's love for you that saved us all from annihilation, not that Frank phrased it in quite that way. But Frank wanted something in return, of course." Dan took a long and final drag on his fresh drink and sat there staring into the scarred surface of the table.

"What?" I asked. "What did he want?"

Dan shifted in his seat and the squinching sound his plastic legs made as they turned in a way my real ones never could sent a little jolt through me. He didn't say anything.

"What?" I squeaked. "What is it?"

Dan toyed with his glass and spoke again in a low, crackly voice. "He promised them you."

"What? What do you mean, Dan?" My beloved, reckless, brave and it seemed incredibly stupid Daddy had promised me to the Tanneh? Huh?

"Frank was so impressed with the way your Daddy loved you - and you weren't even born yet - that he made your Daddy promise you would come back to Tanneh. They wanted to see what would inspire that kind of fierce emotion."

"We were just glad that no one was gonna get annihilated or anything, and by the time we got back we pretty much forgot about it. I mean," he amended, "we made ourselves forget about it. You weren't even born yet, for crying out loud! Anything could happen."

"Anyway, your Daddy and Mamma got married when we got back and then you were born and then we lost your Mamma in that viral plague and I guess your Daddy would have told you about it sooner or later, but he never got around to it and then one day it was too late."

"What about you, Dan?" I asked. "How come you never mentioned it? I mean, it's not like we never had any quiet moments together or anything. You mean to tell me the dreaded Tanneh agree to spare human life in exchange for me and it wasn't important enough to mention?" I was having trouble absorbing this little bit of news.

"And the Tanneh death chop on my ship, Dan, is it just a little reminder?" The mark on the *Linda Rae* was real, even if Dan's story was just a mixture of drink, drugs and bad memories.

Dan grinned. "You got it, kid, only it's not a death cop. There aren't any death chops, that's just some bullshit story the Tannehs made up to scare us with. The mark on your ship is just a message."

"Why do they want me?" I asked.

"Frank just wanted to meet you, I guess," Dan said. "They just wanted to see what would inspire that kind of regard. Frank thought it was the one thing that made the humanoid races worth saving, so I guess he wanted to see you in person. Maybe he didn't realize that love is more common than he thought." Dan's face clouded over. "Or maybe it isn't."

I thought about what being human meant, about all my trips through the black face of the system, with my human memories and human emotions right up there on top of my intellect, squeezing it and shaping it into something that maybe the Tanneh wouldn't understand. I could be the death of my kind. Then I looked at Dan's kind face and saw the tears in his eyes. I was glad I couldn't read thoughts like the Tanneh. It would hurt unbearably to know everything. I liked my ignorance, and I saw this whole thing as one more adventure my Daddy had left for me. Besides, there was no way out of it. I sighed and reached across the table to squeeze Dan's hand. "Hey, cheer up. If I'm not an example of irrational love, then I don't know what is. If that's all they're looking for, I guess I'll do it." My father's daughter, all the way. Now, what about that port inspector?"

Dan laughed. "Oh, him. Well, I think the Tanneh sorta come and go sometimes, short trips that they can stand or something. Anyway, maybe that port inspector was one of 'em."

"Okay, you got the route maps for that sector?" Suddenly I was full of energy and determination, or maybe just too many Zombies.

He nodded. "I knew you'd do it, Cooks."

I'm gonna save the rest of the story for another time, another Zombie in another bar somewhere. I did go back to Tanneh and since we're all still here, the trip was a success. But since no one ever returns from Tanneh, I don't talk about it in public, except to a few close friends like you guys. And the Corp doctors who locked me up, only fortunately for everyone, they didn't believe me.

Remember, every time I tell you guys about some cargo I've run or some big, good-looking Corporation officer who caught my eye - okay, not just my eye - for an evening, think about what might have happened on Tanneh, in a place where everyone was as old as the hills and could hear every thought. And think about what it took to ensure your survival. Oh, and buy me a drink - it's the least you can do.

Vinnie's Cargo

And you thought kitties were cute…

When I asked Vincent Cardoza to sit in as co-pilot for a single shuttle-run from Mare Tranq on the moon to Toshiba on Mars, I didn't think it would turn out to be such a pain in the rump.

For one thing, it was a routine shuttle run of supplies from the big lunar city to the newest mining outpost. For another, Vinnie was a fully-qualified pilot with an up-to-date license and everything. How was I to know anything would happen?

My usual co-pilot, N'Doro, was enjoying a well-earned vacation and little plastic surgery, the result of a bar fight and subsequent lawsuit at Big Red's Palace of Pleasure in Mare Tranq. I missed him - he was more than a co-pilot, if you know what I mean. Hell, I don't even know what I mean, but I missed him anyway.

I could have made the run myself, but the new Corporation regulations were being strictly enforced, and one of them said that if you left the Earth-Lunar runs for any of the outposts, you had to have a co-pilot.

So I got Vinnie. I had seen Vinnie around the usual hangouts - he was tall for a pilot and a little better-looking than most of the men, but he seemed to be a sober, hard-working sort. That alone should have been a tip off.

Anyway, he wasn't my type, but I couldn't really be choosy and it was just for the one run. After all, I didn't want to date him, just get to Toshiba and back.

My shuttle, the *Linda Rae*, was not exactly a state-of-the-art cruiser. It was more like a rust bucket with a semi-functional navigation system and no creature comforts at all. But it was cheap to run and all mine, so every gold credit I made was also mine, all mine. Except when I had a co-pilot, of course. Then it was half mine.

We took on a cargo of supplies at Mare Tranq and I started to get antsy. It was almost lift-off and Vinnie still hadn't shown up. If he didn't arrive soon, I would have to choose between subletting the cargo at a loss to a competitor or running the risk of flying without a co-pilot.

At the very moment when I began securing the hatch, having decided to take my chances and go without a co-pilot, Vinnie came sprinting up the dock with a suitcase and a grin. Well, it was okay for him to grin - he didn't have to make the big decisions. All he had to do was sit in the co-pilot's chair, make nice conversation, and read "Shuttle Monthly."

We got through strap-down and lift off and I set the autocourse for Toshiba.

Vinnie had carried his suitcase onto the shabby, peeling anteway we called the bridge and it was resting at his feet. "So what's in the suitcase?" I asked him. Our shuttle flight was what they called a demon run, a six six six - six hours out, six hours at the outpost, six hours back. A change of clothes or a nightie was hardly necessary.

"Uh, nuthin'," he answered.

Now if he had said drugs, guns, booze, or even if he had claimed boys, women, or Martian sex toys, I wouldn't have been curious any more. He was allowed to smuggle whatever he could carry, and that suitcase was clearly within those limits. But "nuthin" got me curious. Nobody carries an empty suitcase.

"For real, nothing?" I asked.

He nodded. "See? Empty." It was indeed empty. Vinnie-boy was taking an empty suitcase on a shuttle run when a full suitcase of just about anything could have netted him a couple of gold credits.

Okay, I had to know. "Uh, Vin, why?"

He looked at me with that crafty look the less-than-intelligent get when they think they're about to put one over on you but they haven't quite figured out how. "Maybe I wanna bring something back." He was a man of few words, one of his good points, I thought.

"But, Vin, you could have filled the suitcase with something, sold it in Toshiba, then brought back whatever you wanted in it. See?"

Oh, jeeze, he saw, but it was too late - we were half an hour into the trip. His pretty face fell. "Uh, I didn't think of that," he admitted.

I have heard it said that men do not consider intelligence a factor when deciding if a woman is attractive. They go strictly on looks. Women, however, need the reassurance that the person they have chosen to find attractive is also intelligent enough to be worthy of the designation. This idea is only one reason why Vinnie and I did not have anything going on between us, not the most important one, but a deciding factor if we had been the last two people in the universe. One look at Vinnie's handsome, empty face would have convinced any woman that the species deserved extinction.

"Uh, don't worry, Vinnie, you'll know for next time."

He brightened visibly. "Yeah," he agreed with another engaging smile. "Next time!" He sat there smiling and pretty. His jumpsuit, the ubiquitous uniform of nearly all shuttle rats, Corporation and independent alike, fit him superbly, and did I mention that he had muscles in places other than his head? I sighed.

"So," I pressed on to remind him that conversation was the chief duty of a co-pilot, "what are you bringing back?"

"It's a secret," he said. He closed the case and I noticed that he had poked a few holes into it. Air holes?

"Okay," I said, "I don't have to know on this leg of the trip, but you know you're going to have to tell me on the way back." It was the law, written or not, that you didn't smuggle anything on a shuttle without the pilot knowing about it. There was usually no difficulty, as anything could be smuggled, but it was custom and courtesy to let the pilot know what it was. You didn't have to share the profits or the cargo, just the info.

Vinnie got the stubborn look of a little boy who has been ordered to play nice and doesn't want to. If I had been more interested in him or his mystery cargo, I would have poked at the situation until he gave me some kind of reaction. But I wasn't. I went back to my book, an epic about a portable wormhole or some such nonsense. Those late twentieth-century writers were really a trip, and I loved what was affectionately known as "The Golden Age of Science Fiction," even if they did have most of the science backwards.

We were there before I finished the book, but only because I fell asleep in the middle of everything for about an hour. Vinnie was snoring like a disturbed freight train, his little suitcase clutched to his bosom like a favorite teddy bear as the voice of traffic control came through the crackling radio set.

I flew past the main Martian port at Gernsback and kept on to Toshiba, a small domed outpost in the central mining region. I set down at the simple spaceport, got out my paperwork and woke Sleeping Beauty from his slumber. He snorted and grumbled and in general made all those disgusting noises that endear men to the less discerning.

"C'mon, Vinnie," I said, "we've got less than six hours. I'm going to arrange for a nice bit of return cargo. You can go play, but be back here with an hour to spare. That's an hour before lift-off, got it? If you're not back on time, you don't get paid." Sometimes you had to put it in terms they could understand.

He nodded and clutching the suitcase, wandered off in the general direction of the mining operations.

I spent an hour or two negotiating for a small batch of refined pilium ore from a couple of independent miners and then had a pricey dinner in the Corporation casino. I could have gambled away a year's pay in there, but I wisely kept my wallet shut once I saw how the tables were rigged. I figured the food was enough of a gamble for one trip.

An hour before our scheduled departure, I ran all the maintenance checks, put a couple more items on the "fix it when you get rich" list, and wondered idly if Vin had loaded his suitcase with anything dirty or dangerous. Whatever it was, he probably got gypped, I thought.

At precisely fifteen minutes to lift-off, a mere forty-five minutes late, Vinnie came loping toward the shuttle, lugging his little suitcase with both hands as though it were very heavy.

He grinned sheepishly as I held the hatch open for him. "I hope it was worth it," I said. I didn't really intend to dock his pay, but damn it, we had agreed on a time.

"Oh, it was," he said. "I guess I won't really need the pay." He carefully placed his suitcase in a little recess on the bridge and patted it protectively. Then he went to sleep.

I had never, ever, heard a shuttle rat say they didn't need the pay. If Vinnie had come down with Martian fever or something, he was still damn well going to help me pilot back to Mare Tranq. I eyed him suspiciously. He didn't look sick. He didn't look anything but pretty and vacant. And asleep.

I sighed. I did a lot of sighing that trip.

Once we cleared Gernsback and were on auto, I woke Vinnie up and asked him what was in the suitcase. I had a right to know, it was my ship, after all.

He took the suitcase out of the recess and carefully opened it. An egg the size of a football was nestled in an old towel. It looked like an ostrich egg, only there weren't any ostriches at the Toshiba outpost. There weren't any ostriches on Mars at all.

"What is it?" I asked. It had a peculiar pattern, an intricate lacy swirl of pale blue on its creamy shell.

"It's an egg," Vinnie announced proudly.

"Yeah, Vinnie," I said, not bothering to sigh. "An egg of what? What thing laid this?" It looked porcelain. I touched it and it was cool to the touch. It did not feel alive at all. In fact, it felt exactly like a piece of soapstone or maybe ceramic. I had the feeling I was looking at someone's Easter decoration.

"I bought it," he said. "I paid a lot for it, but it's really gonna be worth something when it hatches." He was smiling and fondling the egg in its suitcase nest.

I had a sudden vision of someone paying way too much for magic beans.

"Okay," I said, this time coming very close to sighing. "What's supposed to hatch out of it?" It looked pretty solid, like the only thing on the inside of it was more of the outside. "And don't you have to sit on it or something? You know, incubate it?" If I was going to participate in Vinnie Cardoza's pathetic attempt at smuggling, I was at least going to have some fun with it.

He looked at me with those beautiful brown eyes, the ones in which comprehension was generally absent, batted those perfect lashes and said, "Uh, I don't think I have to with this one," implying there might have been others in the past which required his incubation skills.

The egg, or whatever it was, sure was pretty. I didn't want to know how much Vinnie had lost on it, though. Whatever he paid was his business, bad business though it may have been. I was about to ask him where exactly he had purchased the little treasure when the little treasure began to change color.

"Wow!" I said, "Look at that!" The creamy background was a pulsating red now, and the blue tracery looked more and more like veins. I heard a humming noise coming from it and I reached out to touch it. I could feel the vibrations, but it was still cool, almost cold. It did not feel alive. I wondered if it might be an electronic instrument of some sort, or maybe a decorative or ceremonial item.

Or maybe a bomb.

"Oh, shit, Vinnie," I squealed. "Is it a bomb?" I was a little nervous and excited, but since no one had ever attempted to blow up a cargo shuttle - ever - and since if there was gonna be a first time, it would probably be me blowing up my own shuttle for the insurance, except I didn't have any, but that's a different story, I wasn't exactly panicked.

The egg cracked in a long, jagged diagonal fracture. The noise was crisp, brittle, thin, like the snap of fresh potato chips, and something whitish stuck out of the crack, something sharp.

"What is it?"

"I told you," Vinnie said with his dazzling grin. "Look! It's coming out!"

It was coming out. The sharp whitish thing was a tooth.

"Vinnie!" I shouted, "What the hell is it?"

"Uh, it's a baby," he said. "I told you."

He hadn't told me squat, but that didn't matter. What mattered was that the tooth had broken through the colored, pulsing shell and was making its way up and down the crack, enlarging it. Finally a piece of the shell broke away to expose a snout. The tooth appeared to be growing out of the top of the snout. Weird. It waved back and forth as the snout worked its way out further.

Then a little head appeared. I knew it was a head because, in addition to the snout with the weird tooth on top, it also had two little eyes, lidded with translucent, knobby eyelids. They blinked and the little eyes looked like shiny black beads. A comb or wattle or something grew up from the head, pink and wobbly as the head thrashed around.

A skinny neck stretched out and revealed patches of iridescent green and bits of pimply purple. This was the ugliest baby chick I had ever seen.

Vinnie made little clucking noises at it. The thing turned to look at him, and I swear it gave him a look of exasperation. Then the shell cracked all the way in half and the creature was completely exposed. It looked tiny and helpless and not too chicken-like after all. I wondered if it was some kind of exotic baby crocodile, another species not found on Mars.

Then it unfolded a little pair of wings, shiny and transparent like a fly's wings, and dried them in the shuttle's stale air. It yawned, showing a mouthful of sharp little teeth and a forked tongue. Nope, definitely not a chicken.

"Vinnie, it's a dragon!" I figured dragon rather than dinosaur, because dinosaurs were one more thing Mars didn't have. In fact, Mars didn't have much in the way of lifeforms at all, except for the human colonists, a boatload of bacteria and a couple of native species of reptiles, including a sentient aquatic thing that kept to itself in underground streams. Oh, and the extremely rare and protected thing called a Martian dragon.

The dragons were also thought to be sentient, but as they were so rare, no one had had much of a chance to find out. The Corporation wasn't interested in scientific pursuit that didn't lead directly to profit, so the Martian dragons had become more of a myth than anything else. Until Vinnie got one.

"Vinnie, you can't keep it," I said. I was looking at a piece of Martian history. It looked back at me and made a little squawk, then climbed out of the remnants of its shell and walked rather clumsily around on the shuttle floor.

"He's looking for food," Vinnie deduced, and crumbled up a bit of chocolate from an old candy wrapper in his pocket.

I knew chocolate could be dangerous to some animals, but before I could do or say anything, the dragon darted to it and ate it in one bite. It flapped its little wings and seemed unable to fly, but it was clear that it was hungry. Vinnie rummaged in his pockets for more edibles.

The creature ate Vinnie's candy bars and I got some fruit out of the food locker. It ate that, too, and pushed its little snout into the locker looking for more. I gave it a sandwich and after devouring it, the dragon set about grooming itself sort of like a cat, only without the fur, of course.

"What should we name it?" Vinnie asked, beaming at it like a proud papa.

"Nothing, Vinnie," I said. "We can't keep it! It's endangered! The Corporation will have our guts for garters if we try taking this little guy anywhere. It has to go back to its own planet, for crying out loud." I reset the autocourse for a turnaround back to Toshiba.

"Aw, c'mon," Vinnie whined. "The guys I bought the egg from didn't want it."

"What about its mother, Vin?" I asked. "She missed its birth." I felt sad for the mother whose egg had been stolen, not that I am naturally overwhelmed with maternal instincts. I usually find the young of any species, including my own, to be noisy and smelly.

But I liked the little dragon. It had climbed back into the suitcase for a nap and was fast asleep after the exertion of entering the world and eating its first candy bar.

I reached over and covered it up with the bit of towel. It seemed to purr and I petted its cool, scaly skin as it slept. It sure was a cute little thing.

"Vinnie, we're gonna be in big trouble if we don't get this little guy back where he belongs." I had visions of the Corporation security forces arresting us. Then I had visions of the mother dragon coming after us for stealing her baby. I didn't know which one was worse. I had never seen a Martian dragon before, and I didn't know how big they got. The mother could be one big mother.

"Aw," Vinnie whined. "I'm gonna lose a lot of money on this." His pretty faced pouted.

"You'll lose a lot more than money if we don't get him back," I said. I checked our timer - we had half an hour to Gernsback and then twenty minutes to Toshiba. Not for the first time, I wished for a fancy onboard computer that could call up esoteric information at the snap of a voice command, just like in the videos. What I had instead was an old version of an encyclopedia on my disk. I pulled up all the information I could find about Martian dragons.

When Mars had first been colonized by Corporation mining engineers, a few naturalists had gone along to catalog whatever could be found. The sentient aquatics were located but first contact with them was a disappointment. They didn't want anything to do with us. However, as long as we didn't bother them, they didn't care what happened to the parts of their planet they didn't use, so we built the big base at Gernsback and a few little outposts like the one at Toshiba.

The dragons didn't make themselves known for some time, being the stuff of indistinct sightings and myth for a few years, much like the Yeti Earthside. They seemed to live in a particular area not desirable to the humans for any kind of exploitation. They kept themselves to themselves, and like the aquatics, were thought to be sentient but unsociable. That was it. No habits, language, diet, or other information.

It was strictly forbidden to mess with the natives. The Corporation was very concerned about profit, and a native disturbance of any kind anywhere was cause for immediate Corporation attention and diversion of profit. Anyone responsible for such a disturbance could find themselves relegated to a compost heap on old Earth.

I saw the little spaceport at Toshiba on the screens and set down pretty far from the other traffic. I didn't want too many gawkers and lookie-loos to annoy us as we tried to carefully replace our contraband animal.

Vinnie, whose disappointment about the creature was short-lived when I explained that he could probably make up his losses with the pay he'd receive from the shuttle run, held the creature's sleeping form in the suitcase during our landing, cradling it so that the little monster would not be disturbed. It wasn't. It slept soundly through the whole thing.

We did have a little reception party, however. The two guys Vinnie had bought the egg from were there to greet us, and to offer Vinnie twice what he'd paid, if we would only give the egg back.

"No can do," I said to them. They offered more. Vinnie was about to accept their generous offer when I yanked him back into the shuttle hatch and explained that we couldn't give the egg back because we did not have the egg anymore. "We have the little guy, Vinnie," I said. "We don't have the egg. They are offering money for the egg."

"Oh, yeah," Vinnie said, with his usual handsome and completely blank expression. There was nobody home. I had sighed so much that I was in danger of hyperventilating, but I sighed again. How do guys like

Vinnie manage to stay alive? Can the "pretty" genes have just as much a chance as the "smart" genes?

"You stay here with Junior," I ordered. Vinnie nodded and went to check on the little tyke.

"Okay, boys," I said to the rather shabby pair. I folded my arms and waited.

They exchanged a couple of meaningful glances. "Your partner there bought something from us..." one of them began. They both looked alike to me - worn features, rough hands, dusty old jumpsuits, faces permanently marked by goggles.

"...and aren't you lucky we decided to come back," I finished for him. "Look, you sold him a Martian dragon's egg, which you know is extremely illegal. He brought it aboard my shuttle, subjecting me to some pretty severe punishment if caught. I don't care how you got it, but I do care where you got it. It has to go back, that much you know or you wouldn't be here. But here's the deal. I want to take it back myself." I wasn't a nut-case for danger, I just wanted to see where the little miracle had come from, and if there was a chance of seeing the mother without getting fried to a crisp or otherwise killed. I had been cooped up on shuttle runs for way too long.

The one who had kept silent spoke. "They have lairs," he said. "We got it from a lair. I'll draw you a map. There was nothing else around when we took it, but I've seen the big ones. You don't want to go in there without being warned. The big ones can make you . . . do things."

"What kind of things?" I asked thinking briefly that there had been one or two co-pilots in my day who could make me . . . do things, not to mention a contraband psi box and a homely Inspection Officer once.

"Just, you know, uh, things," he said. I began to wonder if all men in space suffered from some sort of brain damage. He scribbled a map for me, and gave me some general directions.

"Okay, guys, now about the money." Reluctantly, they gave me two gold credits. I kept them in my open palm. "Twice that," I demanded. "I have to take the damned thing back for you." Two more gold credits crossed my palm and closed my fist. "Thanks." I wondered if some of the things an adult dragon could make you do was give back money and get back their eggs. It was likely.

The miners disappeared and I went back inside the *Linda Rae*, where Vinnie was rocking the baby in the suitcase and singing to it. He looked kinda sweet.

I fastened the hatch, put the shuttle in overland mode, and took another look at the map. We were in the designated location in minutes, an empty stretch of reddish rocks and dirt with an impressive mountain range jutting up into the Martian sky. I handed Vinnie a breather and zipped up my jumpsuit, pressing the "outside" button on the left wrist for pressurization. I felt the suit seal on me and put the breather over my head.

The dirt was dry and crunchy under my boots and the baby woke up when Vinnie brought it outside. A pair of gills fanned out on its little head and it blinked a few times, adjusting to the atmosphere. Then it seemed to be okay.

I consulted the map and set out toward the near mountain, a rough-looking spire that poked up dangerously from the uneven ground. As we got close to it, the baby became agitated and tried to jump out of the open suitcase. Vinnie hung on to the little tyke.

I had my Glock Stingray on my belt, and it was set at high stun, in case we ran into trouble, but I had never actually seen a full-grown Martian dragon before, so I didn't know what to expect. I guess I reasonably thought it would be a larger version of the baby.

I heard, or rather felt, her first, a low humming that seemed to resonate through my body. The baby was jumping up and down, flapping its little wings, and making noises.

She was much smaller than I had imagined, standing fully upright at not more than four meters. She had the same general shape as the baby, but her head was differently colored, and she wore a crest or crown of some sort. Her wings were small and transparent, the same wings you'd see on a common dragonfly, and fanned so rapidly they were a blur. I thought the sound must be coming from her vibrating wings. She was not threatening in the least, and when Vinnie set the suitcase down on the ground, the baby raced to her.

She sniffed at the baby and ran a forked tongue over its little head. Then she turned to me and said, as clearly as if she had been speaking Chinglish out loud for most of her natural life, "Thank you for returning the Prince. My people are grateful."

"Huh?" I said with my usual eloquence.

The dragon made a small bow in my direction. "It is not an auspicious beginning, but perhaps it is time for our people to communicate with you more fully."

I got the feeling that this was a moment of great diplomatic import. Swell. Me and Vinnie, interplanetary ambassadors. The Corporation was gonna have a fit.

"Uh, Your Majesty," I said, extemporizing like crazy, "it's our pleasure to return the Little One to you. Boy, he sure is cute. I don't know what got into those guys who stole your egg. That's a definite no-no." I could tell I wasn't using the best diplomatic language, but the dragon seemed to understand.

A few more reptilian heads peeked around the rocks at us and I saw that there were at least a half dozen adults, none of them eager to get very close to us. Maybe we smelled bad to them.

The mother continued. "We will make more formal contact with your leaders shortly, but we would like to request that one of you remain here with us as our guest until then."

"I'll stay," Vinnie volunteered before I could stop him. The mother dragon inclined her head toward him.

I didn't like the idea of anybody staying there, but if a choice had to be made, I'd rather leave Vinnie.

I said good-bye to Vinnie and the mother dragon, and kissed the little tot on his scaly purple head, then went back to the *Linda Rae* and flew overland to Toshiba. I queued up at the spaceport for take-off to Mare Tranq, hoping that the Corporation security guys wouldn't catch me flying a load of refined pilium without a co-pilot.

But I was not so lucky. The Corporation caught me and I was fined all the profits of the trip. One more sigh.

In the end, we never did hear any more from the dragons of Mars. I suspect that once they got to know Vinnie well, they decided that we weren't really a sentient species after all, and voted against making any kind of formal contact.

As for Vinnie, well, sometimes I wonder how he made out, all looks and no brains in a place where his looks weren't worth anything. Or maybe they thought he was cute, too.

CHUMP CHANGE

I once got a rather prim rejection for this story – from a space opera 'zine, no less - citing discomfort with the horny female protagonist. Then I submitted it to a different market where "horny female protagonist" was considered a plus. No accounting for taste…

Even the most sincere declaration of undying affection usually involves a catch, and the declarations issuing from the speaker of my companion were no exception. The catch here - well, there were two catches, actually - consisted of the fact that the companion was a cut-rate heap of metal, plastic and duct tape and also the fact that it was not programmed to express affection.

It was a navigation device, programmed to get my rust-bucket, the *Linda Rae*, from one sector to another without ending up in the uncharted hollows of deep space or the solid interior of some piece of space rock.

Having it tell me it loved me was disturbing on so many levels, but navigational malfunction rather than any sudden feelings it may have unaccountably developed was my main concern.

"Oh, crap," I said to my human companion on the bridge, my co-pilot. "The nav's on the fritz again."

He grunted and reached for his toolbox. N'Doro is six and a half feet of solid, gorgeous hunk. Not the brightest LED on the bridge, but beautiful. I really don't need much more than eye candy as my junk freighter is too small for any real co-piloting but too large to escape the Corporation's picky rules, so I am stuck with the requirement for a co-pilot without actually needing one.

N'Doro fills that bill admirably. Okay, he gets a little rowdy when we are in port, altercations being the natural result of good looks combined with dim wits. But on the road, he is pretty, quiet, and cheap.

Not that we are an item. I usually go for something a bit brighter than N'Doro, but sometimes that's pretty hard to find, so I make out as best I can.

Running a freighter from one outpost to another might not seem like the romantic adventure of a lifetime, but after a stint as a Corporation pilot, it sure has its moments. I'll carry anything that fits – and only the condition of the *Linda Rae* dictates how far and how fast we go. My time as a Corporation pilot stands me in good stead in the outposts. I am still fit, still young enough to look good, and still get mistaken for a Corporation drone when it suits me.

At the moment, however, we were pretty much stuck in Cernan until I could scare us up a cargo run with some advance money to get stuff fixed.

The bars in Cernan are neither the sex palaces of Mare Tranq nor the lavish drug pits of Toshiba Station, but they generally serve up a nice combo of drinks and gels from about a gazillion different places and there's always humanoid company to be found. Not that I am a stickler about the humanoid part.

"Stay, N'Doro," I told him on my way out. "You can hit the bars when I get back, unless I get lucky and we fly." I needed to find some business and for that N'Doro can be a liability. I'm not saying we crash landed on Cernan, but stuff sure did start falling apart just before touch down at the public docks.

Stinky Puffer's isn't quite as bad as it sounds, the name of the place being an inept translation from some local tongue. It smells, like most other places in Cernan, of canned air, plastics, and smoke. The native inhabitants have a sort of smoky odor that tends to permeate the city. I don't find it too unpleasant, but after a few drinks I start worrying that I left the stove on somewhere.

I hit Stinky Puffer's first because it has stiff drinks and a decent ladies' room. After a couple of good drinks, the ladies' room assumes great importance and it's nice if you don't have to share it with garbage, vermin, or men.

I sat at the bar, on the side reserved for pilots, nodded to the others and ordered a local specialty. It was blue and gelatinous and tasted of mint and fresh air and a slight summer breeze, although I knew it was my imagination that supplied the details. I didn't want to know what was in it.

"Looking for company, pretty lady?" The companion droid was configured as a woman, but as I watched, it changed into a reasonable facsimile of a human male. They were clean, safe, and expensive, but after trying one once, the thrill was gone. They didn't actually offer company, but they were programmed to do anything you wanted. Anything.

"Uh, no, thanks," I said. I turned back to my drink. There wasn't much of a crowd, and I didn't want to have to work every bar in town to get a cargo. Usually I have enough fuel and supplies and the *Linda Rae* is in good enough working condition so I can bargain for cargo runs. But this time I was at a real disadvantage and hoping no one would figure that out.

I was facing the decision of whether to buy another drink when a full glass appeared on the bar before me. I pasted on a smile and turned around to see who had bought me a drink.

Just my luck – I hadn't seen Dan Hollifield since junior high. Okay, maybe a bit more recently than that. We flew a Corporation star cruiser together, just the two of us and the thirty or so other pilots necessary to fly something that big. It was a while back, before I walked out and threw in my Corp uniform for a life of well, no uniforms.

That uniform looked damned good on him with a captain's stars on the collar. I tried to remember if I had ever seen him out of it, but frankly, those days were sort of a blur. That can be a good thing.

"Hey, long time…" He waved away a couple of companion droids and brought his drink over, taking the empty stool next to me. "You look great," he said, eyeing my worn jumpsuit and scuffed boots. "You haven't changed a bit."

He wasn't too far off the mark – I had kept my figure. But I had changed. Maybe it didn't show or maybe he was just being polite. After my father died in an accident – or was murdered, depending on who you talked to - I took over his old ship, the *Linda Rae*, and quit the Corporation. Quitting was a big deal as they were pretty much the only game on forty planets, and being a former Corp pilot usually meant you had been bounced out for some grisly reason. Very few just walked.

"Hello, Dan. Nice to see you. What are you doing here?" I meant in Stinky Puffer's, of course. It wasn't the classiest of joints for a Corporation captain.

"Gotta ship in, some diplomats here for a conference. You?"

"I'm looking to pick up a run," I said. Might as well see if he had any leads. "Got anything?" I had my best and perkiest smile on and came close to twirling a lock of my hair.

He leaned forward and studied his drink. It was pink and looked suspiciously like a Tom Collins. He twirled the tiny umbrella stuck in a piece of ersatz fruit. "Uh, actually, I was hoping to find you here. I saw your ship in the public docks and thought maybe you could help me out."

"Me? Help you out? Sure, what do you have in mind?" I was hoping for a cargo run, but if he wanted something else, something that might involve a few credits to fix the ship, I could be interested. He was nice-looking, reasonably clean and humanoid. I've done worse.

"Look, I don't want to talk about it here. Can we go somewhere?"

I thought about that. My ship was not suitable for company, especially with N'Doro aboard. Presumably Captain Hollifield's ship was not suitable, either, what with it being a Corporation ship full of diplomats.

Stinky's seemed like the kind of place that would have a back room, I had just never needed one before. I flagged down a bartender and asked if there was a private room available. The droid displayed a small video of several rooms, including one that looked fur-lined and came with toys.

"Just a quiet place where we can talk privately," Dan explained. The bartender showed us a picture of a small office and Dan nodded.

Once in the room, Dan locked the door and set a scrambler on the floor to prevent anyone from watching or listening. It seemed extreme.

"Uh, no one's gonna walk in on us, and if they do, well maybe they'll learn something."

"Hey, Cooks," he said. No one had called me Cooks in a long time. It was short for Cookie and had a story behind it, one I'm not going into here. "I'm not gonna get you all hot and sweaty. I just want to show you something important."

I was already sweating. "Okay, so talk."

"I found something that I know the Corporation would want if they knew it existed. But I found it and I don't want them to have it, so I want you to take it to Toshiba for me. There's a guy there who can protect it for me until I can figure something out."

"What is it?" The Corp wants anything that's worth anything. And if you work for them, anything you find, produce, invent, or give birth to is automatically theirs anyway. It's how they stay in business, well, one of the ways.

A Toshiba run could be lucrative and who knows, maybe I could do a double run with someone else eager to get stuff to a place like Toshiba.

Dan glanced at the door, checked the scrambler again, and then shot me worried glance.

"Hey, it's me," I said. "Whatever it is, it wouldn't be worth my livelihood, Dan. And I don't steal from or rat out my friends. Ever. You already know that or we wouldn't be here. So it's your turn to relax."

"You're right. I trust you. It's just…okay." He took a breath and stared off into the corner. "A couple of weeks ago everything was fine. Predictable, I mean." He looked back at me. "I like predictable, Cooks."

I nodded. It was one of those things that kept us from ever being more than friends. I like unpredictable.

"Anyway, a few weeks ago I had a run to Earthside. I hadn't been there for years. I had forgotten how dirty, dangerous - and beautiful - it is. You know what I mean."

I knew. The mother planet was quite a place. If you had been born anywhere else, it sorta pulled you toward it. If you had been born there to start with, you never really left. It was an old place, a product of evolution rather than design. The cities were dirty, the politics corrupt and the level of crap in the air made a respirator necessary even for natives. Nothing grew there and it was covered with empty deserts and poisonous seas. But there were a couple of wide open cities that were pilgrimage destinations for half the known universe.

"I stayed in New York in one of the Corporation's big hotels. It was really nice, lots of space, windows, sunrise, the whole bit. We all got the standard caution about going outside, but I just had to, you know? I put on some local clothes and walked around. I found a little place to eat and that's probably where I picked it up."

I backed away. "Uh, you're not carrying anything contagious, are you?" Damn, the last thing I needed was some exotic disease.

"No, no, it's nothing like that. I ordered dinner and just had them bring things, anything the waitress thought was good. She was Earthborn and good company, and she sat with me while I ate. It was a wonderful meal, Cooks. Maybe the best I ever ate. And Tula, that was her name, was charming. She told me stories about the restaurant and her family and how none of them had ever been offworld. Can you imagine?

"After coffee – real coffee from the hydroponics plants – I handed her my credit card. But she asked if I could pay in currency. I was embarrassed to admit I hadn't bothered to get any. She took my card and disappeared into the back of the shop. She was gone so long I became alarmed and thought about all the cautions I had ignored.

"She came back with my card and a receipt and that was that. We shook hands – it's still the custom there, even though it feels unsanitary to me. I didn't notice the coin until I got back to the hotel room to shower."

"What coin?"

"There was a coin stuck to my credit card. I didn't notice it until I took everything out of my pockets. I dumped it all on the counter and saw this coin stuck to my card. I peeled it off, ran it under the sterilizer, and thought I'd keep it for good luck or something. I didn't change any money because

I didn't want to have to learn some local currency, so I had no idea what it was worth."

Earth once had hundreds of currencies, much of it in weird old coins of silver or gold, metals now too common to have the value of rarity. They turned up all the time, mostly as good luck pieces and jewelry, hardly any of them worth more than a credit or two unless they were really old and in museums or something.

"But here's the weird part. I threw it in with my soap and stuff and now they're all new."

"Huh?"

"The soap – you know the little travel packets? I had a couple of them, pretty beat up and one of them almost empty. You know, the usual travel stuff. I threw the coin in my travel kit and when I got back to the ship, everything had been, well, renewed."

"Whaddaya mean, renewed? Someone took out your old stuff and gave you new stuff? That doesn't make any sense, Dan. Besides, a travel kit is worth what, three or four credits, max?" My dreams of major repairs to the *Linda Rae* started to shimmer and fade. Maybe Dan was cracking under the strain of piloting a Corporation cruiser. It happened.

"Cooks, the kit magically renewed itself. And it wasn't just the soap. I threw the coin into my sock drawer. Yeah, you guessed it: new socks. So I tried it in my cooler. I had one bottle of Corp brew in there, but the next time I checked, there was a shiny new sixpack."

My dreams of repairs and a flight outta Cernan with credits in my pocket fizzled, popped and vanished. Poor Dan. Poor me.

"Look, I'm not crazy!" he insisted as I edged toward the locked door. "I don't know how it works, but it does. The thing makes stuff all new."

He jammed a hand into his waist pack and drew out a coin. "It's true, Cooks. Look, here it is."

I took a look. It was silvery, a couple of inches across, and ridged on the edges. The side I was looking at had a picture stamped into it, a large bird of some sort looking over its shoulder, and some writing I didn't recognize in teeny tiny script. Dan flipped it over in his palm – the reverse side looked like a miniature landscape with more writing. It was old and worn a bit. I had seen coins before – almost every world had them, even if they were just ceremonial. It looked like it came from Earth, but I'm no expert.

"Okay," I said. "Pretty coin, old coin. Probably not too valuable unless it really can perform tricks. But Dan, are you sure the coin made those things happen? I mean, are you sure you didn't, you know, forget you had some new socks and maybe someone left you a sixpack as a gift or something?"

He ran a hand over his face and I could tell he wanted me to believe in the coin. "Look, even if you don't think any of it's true, will you at least take it to Toshiba for me?"

"Uh, I'd need the credits in advance, I got a few things to fix on my ship…"

"That's okay," he said, relief in his voice, "Here's half up front, I'm figuring your usual rates and a twenty percent bonus as the item is so valuable. I just, you know, need someone I can trust."

I sighed and put the credits in my wallet. If you can't trust me, well, who can you trust? "Who's the contact on Toshiba?"

"Lester Snipely. He's got the resources to protect the coin and he'll know what to do with it."

Lester Snipely was an old acquaintance of mine. We went way back, back as far as stealing a ship on a pirate run when I still worked for the Corporation. Those were the days. It was nice to know he was still in business. Maybe I could squeeze a little something out of Lester at that end. I smiled. Things were looking up.

Dan's flushed face sported a happy grin. "Okay, Cooks – I'll meet you back here," he checked his chrono, "how about tomorrow? I'm only in town for a few days. Will that be long enough to get your ship ready? I can buy you a drink and give you the package."

"Okay, and thanks, Dan," I said, mentally figuring out the repair schedule. There would be plenty of time to replace my bad systems, get a real bath at one of the fancy bathhouses on Cernan, and still make my date with Dan at Stinky Puffer's.

"Hey Dan," I said as he turned toward the door. "Take care of yourself."

"See you tomorrow," he promised.

I watched him leave. If the gizmo did what he said it did, we were sitting on something really special. People – and I use the term as loosely as necessary in that sector – got killed for a whole lot less all the time. I didn't want anything to happen to Dan, especially with the promise of more credits just for a quick run to Toshiba and a visit with Lester. I had a moment of worry, but then I thought of the work ahead of me and turned it off. Dan was a big boy and I had enough money to get the *Linda Rae* fixed properly.

I went back to my ship, contracted for extensive replacements with the mech bots, paid up front, and let N'Doro hit the town.

I watched some of the repair work, then went back to town to find a good bathhouse. I wanted the works – real water, real soap and a real scrub by someone who knew precisely how to rub a human woman.

I found just what I was looking for and spent several hours getting clean and sweet smelling and remembering what all my personal equipment was for.

With a healthy glow, I returned to the ship in time to see the mech bots haul away the old protesting navigational system and replace it with a state of the art model that took up half the space on the bridge. That made room for a new console. I had plenty of credits, so I ordered a redo on the bridge interiors, something I had wanted for a long time.

N'Doro was still out – I knew I'd probably have to trawl the bars or the local lockup for him in the morning. I had as good a dinner as could be found on Cernan and found a nice, quiet place to sleep. The ship would be noisy all night with repairs, and I wasn't looking for company, so a hotel sounded good.

The next morning I found N'Doro at the third bar I checked and had him hauled back to the ship where he spent a while in the refresher before passing out in the co-pilot's chair. The repairs were finished and the ship looked good. I ran all systems through a shakedown, then moseyed on out to Stinky Puffer's to meet Dan.

Dan never showed.

I waited all afternoon, fending off companion droids and freebie drinks. Finally, I hopped a transport over to the big Corporation dock for a gander at Dan's ship. If he changed his mind, he was out the advance he had given me. It was a sizable sum, though, and I was pretty sure he was determined to get his coin to Lester.

His ship was gone. The mech bots confirmed it had sailed that morning with a full crew, including all the captains.

I was dumbfounded. Dan paid me a lot of money and then took off without a word. That wasn't like him.

I walked back to my ship, a long way, but I wasn't in a hurry. Had the Corp found out about his coin and spirited him away? It wasn't the most unlikely scenario, although it assumed the coin thing was real, and I wasn't ready to believe that yet.

When I got back, N'Doro was awake and the ship looked good. I still had plenty of Dan's money left over and I couldn't wait to get out of Cernan, but I didn't want to leave without knowing what happened to Dan.

Finally, I had to admit there was no reason to stay, so I charted a course for Toshiba. Might as well drop in on Lester and see if he knew anything.

We were pretty far from Cernan when N'Doro handed me an envelope.

"Your friend gave that to me for you. He said to give it to you when we got out of Cernan."

"When was this?" I asked. "What friend?"

"Last night at Stinky's. Some guy, said he knew you."

I opened the envelope. There was nothing in it except a coin, *the* coin, by the looks of it. I turned it over in my hand. Dan must have had an idea that the Corp knew something about his find and took extra precautions.

But that would mean the Corp believed it could do what Dan said.

We had a way to go before we got to Toshiba, enough time to try it out. I put the coin in my wallet with all the remaining credits, my pilot's card, and a piece of stale gum. I figured I could check when we landed, see if my money had magically turned into a fortune. Then I could drop the thing off with Lester. After all, I had promised Dan.

When we landed at Toshiba, I called Lester and set up an appointment, then checked my wallet. Just like I thought – my credits were still the same as in Cernan, and my pilot's card hadn't changed.

The piece of gum, though, had turned into a brand new pack.

I started down the dock to meet Lester, waving when I saw him, but a couple of Corporation security guys were headed toward my ship, so I turned around. Lester saw what was happening; he knew we would meet up eventually.

I had a chance to try out all the new ship's systems as we winked out of that sector in record time.

I knew a million places to hide from Corp drones and laid in a course a long way out of their jurisdiction. I had a spiffy almost-new ship and plenty of money. I also had Dan's coin and a new pack of gum. I put the ship on autopilot and got the coin.

I put it in the cooler and smiled at N'Doro. It was gonna be a long trip. A little extra beer wouldn't hurt.

Back to Tanneh

The trip back to Tanneh changed more than my life – it changed everything.

The tale of that trip back to Tanneh is something I always thought I'd save to tell my grandchildren. Of course, that was when there was a sliver of a chance that I might have some, said chance having gone bye-bye with age. Yeah, I know, I could have child-clones made, even grandchild-clones, if I so desired. You can do almost anything with your own DNA these days. But regular, natural grandchildren? Not a chance as I'd never had any regular children.

Not that any children of mine would have been even remotely classified as "regular" no matter how loose the standards.

Anyway, I always thought I'd be sitting by a simfire with a Zombie cocktail and a couple of little wide-eyed kiddies when I told the tale of the Tanneh trip, not locked down in a Corporation holding facility on unspecified charges with a Corp doctor and a shot of truth serum.

Actually, I had once before been with a Corp doctor and we did play around with some truth serum – a sort of truth-or-dare game – but that was a long time ago and we were both consenting adults. This was completely different, as I was nowhere near consenting to imprisonment and drugs. And the doctor was a woman, or a female of some sort, and not my type at all.

I can only guess how the Corporation found out about my trip to Tanneh. Torture was their usual means of getting information, but aside from the Tanneh themselves – and they don't count because they don't communicate with the rest of the universe - the only other person who knew about the trip was Dan Holly, and he wasn't exactly in a position to spill the beans with or without Corporation inducements.

He wasn't behind the bar at the Mare Inebrium, his retirement fantasy. He was in a high-security institution for the criminally insane on Taureg IV, the result of an unfortunate misunderstanding. He'd been there for quite a while, and was unlikely to get out anytime soon, at least without some help. He was also unlikely to chat to Corp officials on account of being in a coma, the Tauregs' unique treatment for mental disorders. I made a note to check on him. After all, he was my father's closest friend and I suppose mine, too. And the misunderstanding sorta involved me as well, although it had absolutely nothing to do with the unauthorized trip to Tanneh and was really the fault of a Taureg official who didn't understand the concept of free trade.

But I had more immediate fish to fry, what with spilling my guts to the Corporation about the Tanneh trip and what went on there. I guess it all worked out for the best, just like the trip itself, in that we're all still here and not disintegrated for the good of the galaxy or whatever the Tanneh had in their collective mind as a method of humanoid disposal.

However it happened, the Corporation got wind of the trip and promptly hauled me in for questioning. Okay, not too promptly, as the trip in question was years ago – fourteen years to be exact, but I have only been in this Corp holding facility for about a month. So far, I've told them everything they've asked for. It's just that Corp psychs don't always ask for everything. I haven't told them the best part because they haven't asked about it.

Fourteen years can be a long time. If you are young, it can be a very long time, the concept of time being tied to the amount of your total life it represents. Fourteen years is half a life to young person – more sometimes. But to me it is now just a few drops in the temporal bucket, hardly enough to swish around in one's mouth and spit out. Only I remember it all as if it were yesterday.

I even remember before then, I remember getting back from a run more than twenty years ago with a Tanneh death chop on the underbelly of the *Linda Rae* and meeting Dan in his bar – you know the one, where they make those great Zombie cocktails. It's still there, or was not too long ago. I had a package of chocolate krik for him and he had a story for me. He told me about the trip to Tanneh he had made with my father, the trip that supposedly saved us all from extinction the first time around. Tanneh has always been off limits, a pain-of-death place. The inhabitants are very protective of their privacy, and it is a serious offense to even contemplate a trip there. But way back when, Dan and my dad did go there – with a Tanneh emissary, no less – and my dad's love for the as-yet-unborn me is what saved the human race from being swatted like annoying flies by the advanced and telepathic Tanneh.

There was a catch to it, of course. There was usually a catch with all my father's endeavors. This catch was a doozie, at least as far as I was concerned.

I had to make the forbidden trip to Tanneh myself as an adult, presumably to show them all what had inspired his devotion. I put off thinking about it for as long as I could. I even forgot all about it a couple of times. But there was always a reminder – a death-chop etched onto the underbelly of the *Linda Rae* or the same recurring dream for a couple of weeks on end or some other weird happenstance.

I knew it was inevitable. I suspected it would also be terminal.

I made up my mind one day that it had to be done. I was in a do-or-die or possibly a do-and-die mood and for once, the *Linda Rae* was in halfway decent shape. I gave my co-pilot, N'Doro, an indefinite leave, and a handsome bonus, and let my nearest and dearest friends, namely Dan, know my intentions.

"I don't know how to get there," I confessed as we sat at the bar in the Mare Inebrium. "How did you and Daddy find it?"

"We had a guide, remember? Funny little guy we dubbed Frank who has us ferry him all over the known universe. Turned out he was the Lord High Muckety-Muck of the Tanneh. That's what you need, Cookie. A guide. And don't look at me – I'm too old for something like that. Besides, once in a lifetime is my Tanneh limit, and that's more than anyone else is allowed. Except you, of course. Jeeze, Cooks, I wish there was some other way." He sighed and looked out at nothing, running the regrets of a lifetime through his head.

"Well, how am I supposed to find it, then?"

Dan sipped a grisly-looking concoction while I stared at my Zombie cocktail. He furrowed his brow in thought, then looked up. "I can give you our charts and everything, but they won't be much help. They'll get you to the right sector, but that's all. I think when you're ready, they'll send someone for you, the way they sent someone to escort your Daddy and me. I think you'll get your own Frank. You just might not recognize him at first."

It sounded plausible, well, as plausible as anything that had to do with Tanneh. It meant I only had to wait and my Frank, like a fabled prince in a little girl's fairy tale, would someday show up. Well, I was good and ready, so where was Prince Frank?

"Gotta go, Cooks," Dan said suddenly. He looked tired. He should have gone home and taken it easy, put his plastic legs up or something. He should have at least kept a low profile, but he was planning that fateful run to Taureg IV. Life is full of "if onlys" but some of them are a damned shame. I wish I could go back and distract Dan from that run. I probably could have done it, too, back in those days. If I have any regrets at all about my life, that's the one.

Me, I was planning a long wait for a guide to Tanneh. Well, it had already been a pretty long wait, but maybe time scrolled differently for the Tanneh and to them I was a just an anxious kid waiting for the Christmas that was months away. Or maybe they had already decided to liquidate the populations of the universe and once again bask in the peace and quiet an empty sector could give a telepath.

Maybe they had forgotten all about it. There was an idea with some appeal. Only I knew they hadn't. Their death chop was on my ship, etched into the hull. I had long since stopped losing sleep over it, but it was a constant reminder that someday something would happen.

Lots of things happened, of course, but no Tanneh. N'Doro came back and we flew twenty worlds with thousands of cargoes, some of them legal, but most just on the edge. We took on passengers of all types, anyone who could pay could go anywhere we could fly. We usually stayed a couple of stops ahead of any nosy Corp types, but once or twice we had to high-tail it out of some tight spot with a handful of credits and an iffy something stashed in the hold. Once, oh, years before any of this stuff, we even delivered what I honestly believe was a magic coin, although that's a story no Corp doctor would believe.

Funny how something really important can happen but you don't really see how important it is until after it's all over. That's how it was when we dropped into Cernan for a layover on the way to Toshiba. It had been a long time since we had sped outta there with a nifty bit of contraband, Corp Security on us like scales on a D'rrish, so things were pretty much the same as on any trip. N'Doro got shore leave and promptly hit the bars, I went off in search of a bath and a nice dinner, and we both knew we'd end up back on the bridge of the *Linda Rae* with a pocketful of credits and a trip to take.

But while lounging in the clear, flower-scented waters of a warm tub, I heard a voice.

"Cookie. I'm waiting for you."

"Uh, I'll be out in a minute," I said aloud. "Wait, who are you?"

There was no answer.

"Hello? Look, if you need the room, I'll be out in a sec. I musta lost track of the time." Baths were expensive and strictly timed and I had only paid for a standard thirty-minute soak.

But there was still no answer.

I got out anyway, dressed, and paid and headed over to Stinky Puffer's, the kind of joint a nice girl like me shouldn't even know about, much less frequent. Hell, they even know me by name, and a companion droid brought me my favorite drink before I had even chosen a seat.

One thing I liked about Stinky's, maybe the only thing, as it really did smell bad in there, was that the dregs of twenty worlds could often be found there, ready to do a little business. It was there that I had last seen Dan in his fancy Corporation pilot days, before the accident that took his legs. He was an ornery cuss about that – he could have had his legs regenerated in less than a week, but he insisted on being different. I wonder what the Tauregs made of his legs. And his metallic voice.

I figured if I made myself visible in all the usual places, Prince Frank or a paying customer would find me. Either way was good, but I felt an inexplicable urgency to get started on the Tanneh thing. It was a strange, gnawing sensation.

"Cookie, I'm waiting."

I turned around, but saw no one. The place had a light crowd, but I was at the bar reserved for captains and pilots, and I was the only one there.

"Me too," I said aloud. "I'm ready when you are." I was ready for a lot of things, a customer with credits, another drink, a few answers, even Prince Frank. Especially Prince Frank.

"Then let's get started."

I spun around again, and again, nothing. No one. Empty spot, except for me.

"Look, I can't really do this invisible voice thing," I said. "If it's time to go, fine. But if we're going where I think we're going, I gotta see you."

"I'm at your ship."

Okay, now we were getting somewhere. I paid my tab and headed out to the public docks. The *Linda Rae* was waiting; the scorch marks of a Tanneh Death Chop barely visible now with the passing of years. It had never attracted much attention – except mine, of course. I wondered about it at first, but like a tattoo on my back, I forgot it was there. For some reason, other people, port inspectors, Corp Assessment Officers, the usual drones with their hands out for bribes, none of them seemed to notice it. That was a good thing.

I left N'Doro a message that he could take his time, that I had booked a quick run and would be back soon. I know, it wasn't exactly true. The quick run might be the rest of my life, or the rest of humanity's existence, or a delightful combination of the two. Whatever it was, it probably wasn't going to be quick. But N'Doro was a good co-pilot, a handsome, steadfast and simple guy, and he deserved to have harsh truths hidden.

I paid the local bribes, had the mech bots do a once-over and ran the engines through a pre-flight test. Everything checked out. All I needed was Prince Frank.

"I have been here all along," the voice said. It was then that I got that prickly feeling that maybe I wasn't hearing Prince Frank at all, that maybe the voice was in my head and I had gone over the edge. Oh, crap, I thought. A nice dose of schizophrenia in the morning. Just what I needed.

"No, Cookie, open your eyes. I am here, really here."

I did the opposite, of course. I shut my eyes tight and shook my head. When I did open them, I was still on the bridge of the *Linda Rae*, but a shimmery form was winking off and on beside me. It stabilized into an opalescent thing about the same shape and color as the inside of a jellybean after you have sucked all the colored shell off it. Larger, though – it was about four feet tall. Terrific. Now I was hallucinating large candy, and minus the really good part at that.

"Are you the delicious candy center?" I asked.

The opalescent form coalesced further and took on a roughly humanoid shape, with a round head, stocky body and wizened little arms and legs. The face of a thousand-year-old baby completed the picture. It – he – made a bow.

"I am Prince Frank," he said solemnly.

I burst into a giggle. His Highness smiled broadly.
"Humor," he said. "I think I get it. But you will need to help me. I can feel what you feel, hear what you think, but I do not have the cultural contexts in which to enjoy it as you do. My real name would not be of use to you, but the name you have chosen will suffice. Now it is time to go."

He climbed into the co-pilot's seat, looking as if he would greatly benefit from a child carrier, and strapped himself in. I sighed, punched up the coordinates for a quick jump to space, and held on.

The original *Linda Rae* was not designed for Deep Space. She was designed for ferrying various cargos from one miserable shithole to another, generally under the radar. But the current version, the product of many successful if not quite legal ventures, was space worthy. The charm of the original rust bucket left to me by my father was still there in the faded upholstery and duct-taped consoles. A Tanneh Death chop was emblazoned on her belly, but her guts were state of the art and her heart was all mine.

It gave me a thrill every time I felt the engines roar into life and then saw the screens go blank for that split second of nowhere before we ended up outside the orbit of wherever we had been. The screens popped on and the field of stars that was my real home winked a welcome.

"Okay, Your Highness, where to?" I needed to set a course of some sort or we would just hang in space.

"You need not worry yourself, Cookie. The course is already set and we will be home shortly. And please stop worrying that your life will be prematurely ended. We have no intentions of harming you."

I thought about my father and Dan, how terrified they must have been, and how relieved. I made a promise to myself to look Dan up once I got back and tell him everything. Funny how the promises you make to yourself are the ones you keep. I tried to keep that one. I didn't know then that things would turn out so badly for him.

Anyway, the trip to Tanneh was uneventful. Prince Frank chatted a bit, but it was clear that maintaining a corporeal presence and speaking was tiring for him, so I suggested he go to sleep or whatever and rest up until we arrived. He dissolved into a mist in the co-pilot's seat and I read an old issue of Shuttle Monthly, then did a safety check. Everything was okay, so I turned the console lights down and tried to snooze myself. I must have dozed off because I remember dreaming about Dan and that bar he loved. And frin juice, the real thing. It was a good dream.

When I awoke, we were nearing Tanneh and the Danger light on my console – broken for several years, and who wants a Corp Danger light wired in anyway - was flashing like a new gold credit. I didn't have time to wonder how or when it got fixed as my screen filled with the Forbidden Planet and the autolanders took over.

We landed safely on a large flat thing that looked like a mile round marble pancake. It was eerily quiet when the engine hiss stopped and I glanced over to see if Prince Frank was awake and solid. He was there all right, but just a jellybean center, no real body. His voice came through my head rather than my ears.

"Cookie, we are home."

Okay, I admit to a nomadic existence where the concept of home is usually the *Linda Rae*, or sometimes the Mare Inebrium on Bethdish or even, sadly, sometimes Stinky Puffer's in Cernan. It never included Tanneh.

But maybe Prince Frank just meant that *he* was home, and that made sense and put me at ease, too.

"No, Cookie, this is your home now, too." Oh, crap – I forgot he could hear my every thought. Oh, well, honesty is the best policy, not that it ever much worked out that way for me.

"Well, then I guess you already know how I feel about that. So, am I a prisoner here?"

"Cookie, you are not a prisoner. You are a welcomed and honored guest who may choose to call our humble planet yours."

I blushed. I'm not sure how that bit translated to Prince Frank through his hear-all, know-all faculties. "Oh. I see, I-uh, I'm sorry, thank you." Then I remembered that everyone on Frank's planet could hear everything I said, thought, or felt. I was an open book to a whole race. I wanted somehow to live up to their expectations, to do my own race proud. But I could only be what I was.

That seemed to be enough.

The marble pancake, which had looked so completely empty when we landed, was full of Frank's people. Most of them were invisible to me, but a few were in that jellybean state and I could see them as candy-like blobs. I could only hear them in my head when they directed their voices at me, but they could hear or feel or whatever my slightest thought. I seemed to be a novelty, but I knew that such novelty could wear pretty thin in a short time. If I were them, I guess I'd wipe us all out for some peace and quiet, too.

I had no sooner formed this thought than I heard Frank give his people a big "I told you so!" He turned to me and materialized to his fullest extent. He looked so old and frail, I just wanted to pick him up and carry him around.

"Cookie, you are your father's daughter."

I smiled. I sure was.

"It was the depth of his feeling for you that intrigued us. But we felt it from his friend, Dan, too, to a lesser degree. Now we feel it from you to all of us. The noise of your thoughts is distracting and annoying, but it is your empathy, your ability to feel emotion for others, even others whom you do not know and cannot know, that is the remarkable thing. We were right to wait for you."

This sounded like good news to me and it pleased me that they had found something worthwhile about me. I admit to being scared it would all turn out badly, with me the main reason humanoid life disappeared in that sector or maybe all sectors, of the universe.

"But there is more."

I sighed. I knew it. Prince Frank gave me the good news first to soften the blow of the bad news. It was an old trick – let' em know what a great job they did just before you fired 'em. That way, they were still basking when the sun disappeared.

I waited for the sun to disappear – or whatever awful thing might happen. The chances of the sun actually disappearing were fair to middling, as far as I could tell, so I braced myself.

"Cookie, it is very difficult for me to maintain this corporeal form. May I disintegrate?"

Now that was polite if I ever heard it. "Of course," I answered as he shimmered a bit then went into his jellybean form before winking out altogether.

"That's better," his disembodied voice sighed. "And it is also part of the dilemma the Tanneh are facing. It's why we called you to come now. We want to make you a proposal, but I think you might be tired and hungry, and we have prepared a place for you to rest and eat, so we will talk after."

"Okay," I said. I was hungry, that's for sure. And maybe I was just a bit tired, too, although sleep would probably be out of the question what with all the excitement of having survived nearly a whole hour on Tanneh.

The marble pancake grew a pavilion and Frank's voice led me to it. Inside there were tables heaped with food and drink and I felt the presence of dozens of jellybean forms, all bustling about with a benevolent regard for my comfort. I could hear them in my head when they addressed me, whispery cooings urging me to eat and be comfortable. I took them up on their offers and seated myself at a table where a whole roast turkey – a real one, mind you – carved itself. Okay, it didn't really carve itself, but as I could not see the hands that carved it, it was almost the same thing. It was delicious, a wonderful treat. Turkeys are only found in the agrarian colonies, and are rare as all get out. Just like the frin juice that sparkled in a beaker in front of me.

"Frank," I said between mouthfuls of turkey, stuffing, mashed potatoes and gravy, "this is just fabulous." A six-layer chocolate cake sliced itself for me, a dollop of ice cream melting over the fudge icing. I dug in.

"We are pleased that you like it, Cookie." Frank sounded pleased, and I radiated my pleasure like a warm cloak.

Even now, under the syringe of a Corp doctor, in a high-security facility on the backside of nowhere, the memory of that dinner can make me smile.

"Frank, the dinner was the best I've ever had, but I'm not really tired. I think we'd better talk about whatever is bothering you."

"Ah, Cookie, please do not distress yourself. If you would like to rest…" the décor switched from feast table to nighty-night and a bed with snowy white sheets. It looked very inviting.

"Well, maybe just for a few minutes." That turkey was doing its job and I felt like a nice little nap. I lay down and the jellybeans covered me with a light blanket. I was out and snoring in seconds.

I don't know exactly what happened while I slept. Obviously, nothing dire or I would be telling the tale, but I know when I awoke, I felt energized and refreshed and I haven't been sick a day in my life since.

Frank was there, his form just barely shimmering. I yawned and sat up. "I feel great," I announced.

"Cookie, you look great. Is that the right response?"

"You bet, Frank. That is certainly the right response. You know, you could get the hang of this humanoid life if you gave it a try."

I could feel him smile. Okay, I couldn't see a grin on his wizened and hazy little puss, but I could feel it. I kinda liked being able to feel his thoughts, at least when he wanted me too.

But I felt a twinge of concern as he sat down beside me on the bed, which had somehow reconfigured itself into a sofa. I couldn't tell if it was my uneasiness or his.

"Okay, Frank, time to talk. Whatever it is, let me just say that you have been really nice to me and I appreciate it no matter what happens now." It was true. My Daddy raised me to be polite, which means not only knowing my manners but also knowing when to use them.

I felt brave and apprehensive and resigned, all at once. It must have taken all of Frank's concentration to wade through the mud of my confused thoughts.

"Long ago we were a great race," Frank began, and I could see this was going to be a serious talk, so I got all settled and comfy and ready to pay attention. "We occupied more than just this planet, we held nearly forty worlds in this sector, all either conquered peacefully and cooperatively or terraformed, as you would say, from barren rock. We valued our peace and our prosperity, and were a vigorous people.

"We were of sturdy bodies in those early days, much like yourself. We could always communicate without voice, though this ability became more pronounced as our physical selves became less important. Millennia ago we knew the time would come when we would lose our physical presence altogether and our existence would be defined only by thought.

"When your father and his friend visited us, it was an opportunity for us to assess your kind. Yes, we wanted peace, the quiet peace that comes of not hearing the incessant chatter of billions. But we also wanted to see if any were worthy of our gift. If none were found, then the gift would not be given and we could then consider other ways to further ensure our quiet existence.

"We were fortunate in what we found, and I think everyone will benefit. But Cookie, it is time for our offer to be formally made. Are you ready to consider it – for yourself and for the whole of your kind?"

Uh-oh, I thought. An offer for myself and the whole of my kind? How could I speak for everyone? What if I had to choose extinction, because, well, so many of us deserved it? I sighed. Yeah, I would do it if I had to. I knew I would also stay right there for the rest of my days if I had to, if it meant that no one else need ever know how close they came to being swatted out of the universe like a swarm of gnats.

"I'm ready," I lied, and I thought I heard the echo of endless sighs.

Frank smiled, his warmth covering me like a soft blanket. "Cookie, we wish to offer you our planet. We are reaching the stage in our development where a corporeal presence is just too difficult to maintain. Once the last of us has made the transition to pure energy, we will no longer have any use for a permanent home world. Already many of our other worlds are inhabited by creatures similar to your kind, creatures who have never even guessed at our existence. But this world, Tanneh, is special to us, Cookie. We would not have our race forgotten, nor our home world merely exploited for its resources, at least not too soon. We want you to become the keeper of all that we hold dear, to watch our world for us, to govern it and maintain our history."

I'm afraid my mouth opened and I just sat there looking like an idiot. The Tanneh wanted to give me their world? Their planet? Me?

"Uh, Frank, I don't think I'm…"

"Cookie, please consider it. It would mean so much to us to know our home world is in your hands. We know you would always do the right thing."

No one had ever had that kind of confidence in me. And I wasn't sure it was a good idea. I mean, if the Corp ever got wind of it, they'd be all over the place.

"Cookie, don't tell them." Frank's voice made it all seem so easy. "You may choose to live here, if you wish. We will provide handsomely for you and you need never lift a finger. Or you may come and go at will. All we ask is that for the duration of your lifetime, you protect Tanneh. We do not ask that the planet become an immutable shrine, my dear, only that for a short while it be undisturbed. We are changing daily and soon we will not be confined to any one sector of the universe. Our homeland will be a fond memory, but that, too, will someday fade."

Nothing is forever. I know that. Not me, not my ship, not even the worlds we live on. But I couldn't promise what I couldn't do.

"Frank, I'm just one person. I can't promise this. I don't know anything about your history, or how to preserve it or even how to get here and back. You need someone strong, determined, and smarter than me."

I felt the warm grin, but this time is was from all of them. It felt like butter, like honey, like sunshine…

"We have chosen correctly."

I sighed. "What if I say no?" I asked, maybe not aloud. But I knew the answer. If they couldn't find a babysitter, they'd have to make sure my kind would not be poking around too soon. The easiest bet would be the peace-and-quiet route of complete annihilation of the humanoid races. I thought about it. Maybe that would best. We sure were an unruly, unpredictable, messy lot; maybe it would be better for the universe if we weren't in it.

"It's part of your charm, Cookie. We don't want to do it that way. We want you."

"Well, if it's what you guys really want, I guess I'll do it. When do we start?" What did I have to lose anyway? I'd miss my ship, and Dan, of course, and maybe N'Doro and yeah, even Max's on Bethdish and Stinky Puffer's on Cernan. I had grown used to my life. But hey, it was for the good of my kind and more importantly, for Frank and his folks. I mean, they sure did have a lot of confidence in me, no matter how misplaced it might be. And I kinda liked the little critters.

So Frank and the others guided me through their history and showed me the library on the marble pancake and I spent what felt like a beautiful summer learning all about the Tanneh and their homeworld. I came to appreciate not only the beauty of the place, but also the quiet. Time moved differently there.

Beyond the marble pancake, which was actually a city if you looked at it in the right light, there were all the usual pretty places, woods and streams and an ocean or two, and as they had been transitioning to their ghost-like selves for a long time, there wasn't anything that needed any sort of maintenance. Even Marble Pancake – its real name was something I never did get the hang of – was pretty much self-sufficient and the power of their sun ran whatever required it.

But even Eden must have gotten a bit boring after a while and I longed to go back to my own worlds, even if just for a visit. I hiked out to the *Linda Rae* one day and just sat on the dusty bridge. I breathed in the stale air as a tear stole down my cheek.

Frank the ever-understanding knew I needed to go home. He could feel my unease, and he recognized it for what it was – homesickness, something I had never really had before as I had never really had a home.

"Cookie, you have done well. It is time for you to go back to your own."

It was exactly what I wanted to hear.

"I'll be back," I promised. "And you'll see, I won't let anyone bother you here or do anything bad to your world." I really meant it, too. In fact, I had a plan.

Frank smiled in my head, and I felt the warm glow of all his people under my skin. I smiled back and got ready to leave.

Well, time gets away. There were jobs when I got back, N'Doro was out of jail and ready to fly, and the excitement of being a pilot with nowhere to go but to the next adventure swept me into its arms. I got swept into a few other arms as well, and it really does all come back to you no matter how long you've been gone, which in my case – although it felt like several months – turned out to be less than a week.

Time sorta softens things, too. It wasn't long before I let Frank and Tanneh become another fond memory. I know I promised, but my great plan was to just do nothing and let Tanneh rest in its glorious isolation. After all, it had worked well for a long time and there was no reason to go stirring things up by bragging about my trip.

I did tell Dan, though. He deserved to know. He sat wide-eyed as I told him all about it, then let out a slow soft whistle when I was done. "Jeeze, Cooks, they made you their queen?"

"No, of course not. Haven't you been listening? I'm just a sort of steward of their homeworld, you know, a caretaker. All I have to do is keep all of us away from it, but I don't think I have to work very hard at that. No one ever has to know I survived a trip there and back, so no one has to know it's safe."

"What about taking care of their history?"

"Yeah, I thought about that. But if no one goes there, no one needs to disturb their archives and their history will stay there until, well, forever."

Dan stood me to a drink and I hugged him. "Gotta go, Dan – I got a run out to Toshiba, then a possible to Otherside. You take care of yourself. I guess we're the only living humans to ever make the trip and back, so that makes us pretty special, but we can't ever talk about it."

"Don't worry, Cooks. Hell, no one would believe us anyway."

I knew he was right. I spent the next fourteen years forgetting it even happened.

Then one day I heard about Dan getting caught on Taureg IV and was minding my own business in Cernan, quietly thinking about how to get him out of there with his head unfried, when a Corp dock inspector cuffed me to the outer railing of my own ship and called in for a reward. I almost laughed at him. Not only was I not wanted for anything, there would definitely be no reward if I were.

But the call was answered immediately with a cruiser full of uniformed cops and a couple of doctors with syringes. I woke up in a Corp holding facility with a headache and an interrogator.

I didn't panic. Well, okay I panicked a little, but when they started asking about Tanneh I was just puzzled. I couldn't lie – the truth serum worked – but I didn't have to elaborate and this felt more like a fishing expedition. If they had been serious about charging me with a crime, they could have asked about any one of dozens of semi-legal trips I had made. But they were only interested in what I knew about the Tanneh, specifically if I had met any. I told them I had probably met a few as I was convinced they walked among us. I told them I thought I had met Prince Frank, but it had been years ago. I told them I didn't know any Tanneh currently. The doc made a lot of notes and shook her head.

She never did ask me if I had ever been to Tanneh.

She was very interested in Prince Frank, though. She wanted to know what the Tanneh looked like, so I told her the truth, that they were invisible. She wanted to know how they communicated with me, so I told her the truth, through the voices in my head. She wanted to know why they had chosen me to communicate with, so I told her the truth, because my Daddy had loved me a lot.

This went on for about a month, then they gave me a ton of medications, suspended my pilot's license and kicked me out.

Dan was right – they didn't believe me. They thought I was crazy. I never did tell them that I had been to Tanneh or that it was safe to go there, and I am so glad of that, but the whole experience got me to thinking about how close I had come to endangering the Tanneh homeworld. I couldn't take that chance again.

Epilogue

For over fourteen years, their secret had been safe, but now I knew I could be a threat. It was only a matter of time before some hotshot at the Corp Psych joint figured out I was telling the truth and got nosy. Well, nosier.

I didn't have a license, and N'Doro had borrowed the *Linda Rae* while I was in the loony bin, so I holed up at Stinky Puffer's and waited for him to get back. I went over all the possible ways to spring Dan from Taureg IV, but I came up empty. I'd have to get there first, then get into a high-security prison, get Dan out and back to reality, and we'd both have to make a getaway. Maybe when we both were younger, we could have done it. But it looked like Dan would breathe his last there. As for me, I'd have to go back to Tanneh to end my days or risk messing that up, too.

Even in a swell joint like Stinky Puffer's things can look pretty bleak.

I was at the bar when a companion droid sidled over, offered its charms and backed off when I waved it away. They were too pricey for me and besides, I wasn't in the mood.

"Since when are you not in the mood?" A handsome pilot with a Corp look about him sat down next to me. He looked good, smelled even better, and almost distracted me.

"Pardon?" Had the guy just read my thoughts? And if so, by whose permission?

"Cookie," he said with a grin, "it's me, Frank. Prince Frank to you."

Wow, that killer grin, that gorgeous body in a pilot's uniform, who was he kidding?

"No, really, Cookie it's me. Do you like it? I don't have to ask, I can feel that you like it very much. Cookie, you are making me blush."

A blush did indeed creep across that handsome face.

"Frank, is it really you? How did you do this?" The last time I had seen Frank, he had been too weak to hold a misty jellybean form together, much less that of a six-foot dreamboat.

"We have learned much, Cookie. Freeing us from our half-life on Tanneh was the best thing that ever happened to us. We are very grateful to you. Although many do live a quiet, contemplative, and ethereal existence among the stars, some of us have learned to embrace the exuberance of humanoid life," he grinned, "with some restrictions, of course."

It was my turn to blush. "But..."

"I'm sorry to have arrived so late. I knew you were in no real danger, though. You can only tell them what they ask and they ask so badly. Had that doctor even come close to asking anything too awkward or hurting you in any way, I or another of my kind would have suggested she ask something else. We were close enough to listen and intervene if necessary. I must say, you did very well on your own."

"So you just let them drug me up and interrogate me?" I wanted to be indignant, but I couldn't. "Aw, I can't stay mad at you, but you already know that. So what's up next? I figured I'd better get on back to Tanneh and live out my life there, you know, to keep it safe."

"It's not what you really want, though, is it, Cookie?" He looked at me with beautiful brown eyes – or were they blue? – and knew what I knew. I wanted my old life back.

"I can't have it back, though, can I? I'm older now."

"Ah, Cookie, you still have a few years left to roam the planets, maybe even the stars. You must do it. You must get your old ship and continue your life. Then, when you really want to, you can come home to Tanneh."

"Really?" It was what I wanted. And the thought that at the end of it all, maybe when I started to feel my mileage, the *Linda Rae* and I could both retire to beautiful Tanneh, well, that sounded pretty good. There was only one thing that kept me from being happy about it, though.

Dan.

"Cookie, we can help him. We can take him from the Taureg and settle him on Tanneh. He is a fugitive, after all. But don't worry, he will be comfortable and you may visit him anytime. And do not worry about your pilot's license. You will find the Inspector at the Public Dock is ready to give it back to you. So you see? Everything has worked out for all of us."

I hugged Frank. It was delicious. He found it interesting, but not in the same way I did. It was a slight disappointment. "Are you sure you can't…"

"I'm sorry, Cookie, some aspects of the humanoid experience are simply not for the Tanneh."

That was the last I saw of Frank. But I never forgot him and even though I always planned to go back to Tanneh, well, what happened instead is another story.

The Spiral Sea

I had just finished this story when Jack Eagan, editor of The Spiral Seas Magazine, asked if I had anything for him. Boy, did I.

My Daddy taught me to fly a shuttle when I was a kid. He didn't have any boys, just one girl, me, so I learned everything I could from him before his untimely death either at the hands of space pirates or in the bed of his partner's wife, depending on which story you believed.

I ran a contract rust-bucket from the big lunar base at Mare Tranq to Otherside Station on, you guessed it, the other side of the moon. It was the sort of exhilarating job one normally associates with snoring, since the main excitement was greeting a batch of dull-headed miners, ferrying them either to or from their place of employment, and then doing it all over again. Ad infinitum. It was a chance to see the same two places repeatedly until they started to look exactly alike.

And the pay-- why, you could almost afford enough to eat on the magnificent salary paid to shuttle rats.

But you already know all about that. About the only thing the job had going for it, besides being steady employment in a place where the unemployed were shipped back to earth for compost, was the chance to make a few bucks on the side carrying exotic cargo for the very rich and/or very perverted.

So how could you blame me for taking the bait?

Mare Tranq had one advantage over Otherside and that was the fact that it was the oldest and most wide-open of the lunar settlements. It was practically a city, for Chrissakes, with buildings that had floors above and below the lunar crust line. And businesses - not everything in Mare Tranq was owned and operated by the Corporation. Independent operators of every sort could be found in the twisting alleyways and dimly lit sex parlors.

"Hey shuttle rat, how's about a business deal?" This from the hulking form of a recent immigrant from earthside. I didn't look at him too closely.

"No, thanks," I said. I had an appointment to get some almost decent food and nothing was going to get in my way.

"Well, how about I throw in something extra?" The voice sounded pleasantly accommodating, and I could have used the money, but the body that went with it had moon-smell, that peculiar body odor earthsiders develop before they learn to bathe with the limited water supply. I gagged and tried to pass him but he blocked my way.

"Hey! Maybe we could talk about a little cargo transaction. Where you run?" The questions sounded like a formality. This guy looked at me as if he were comparing me to a recent photograph.

I breathed through my mouth. "Otherside."

"Shall we find someplace cozy to talk?" His eyes sparkled with anticipation.

"No." I'm always open to business except when I'm hungry and it stinks. I turned around and started heading purposefully toward Wu's Kitchen, the lunar equivalent of Chinese food, equivalent being a very loose term in Mare Tranq.

"Wait! I can pay you a lot!" The voice now had a desperate edge to it and the sparkle had turned to panic.

I stopped, turned around, held my nose, and said, "Look. I don't mind talking business but I am hungry and you smell bad. So I'm going to get some food while you either go get a bath or otherwise disappear. If you opt for the bath, there's a public bathhouse two streets over and I'll be at

Wu's Kitchen for at least an hour and a half. Otherwise, nice talking to you and get lost."

He blushed, no shit.

Public baths aren't cheap, and as I sat at a corner table at Wu's and poured a little more Sirichie hot sauce over noodles of suspect origin, I figured the guy wasn't going to waste good money on a bath. Most of 'em didn't.

But as I sipped the grain tea while deciding between sweet-and-sour-mystery meat and household pet-kung-pao, I saw him. He was still bulky, too much so for most lunar professions, but he was dressed in the usual jumpsuit of a native and looked freshly scrubbed. His shining face was shaven and I could almost smell the soap over Wu's combination of garlic and disinfectant.

He caught my eye and grinned, then raised his left arm, dramatically sniffed his armpit, nodded approvingly and waltzed over to my corner. "I smell great!" he announced. "Now can we talk?"

I gestured with my chopsticks to the chair beside me. My mouth was full, so I just nodded, swallowed, and smiled. I had never, not once, had anybody go to the expense of a bath just to talk.

"So what's your deal?" I asked cautiously.

Okay, I wouldn't have been interested in anything too dangerous or too illegal or too immoral. That last part means anything that would turn my stomach. But if it was something just slightly one or the other and paid handsomely, well, then, show me the deal. And I wanted to know why he had gone to the trouble of a bath just to talk to me. There were hundreds of other shuttle pilots around who wouldn't have been quite so picky.

He looked at my food, waved the waiter away, and leaned in conspiratorially. "I need someone who can fly to Otherside and take something in for me without attracting a lot of attention, someone who comes and goes unnoticed."

Well, it was certainly flattering to know that even complete strangers considered me unworthy of notice.

"What is this something?" I asked, ignoring the compliment. "Just generally, I mean, don't get too specific." If it was something really bad, I didn't want to know the details.

"My sister," he said. He smiled a sweet smile. He wasn't too bad looking, if you got over that moon standard of good looks that demand human beings weigh thirty percent less than the insurance tables hope for.

Wait a minute. This guy was willing to bathe in order to talk me into flying his sister to Otherside. Commercial

Corporation hops were available to Otherside, new shuttles with all the modern conveniences, like upholstery and a working bathroom, and as long as she was even remotely human, she could get a ticket, fly in, and go unnoticed. You didn't need a rat like me flying on an expired transport license in an ancient can of bolts and duct tape.

"So what's wrong with her?" I asked. It wasn't polite, but it seemed nicer than asking him right out what was wrong with *him*. Like where was his brain, for starters.

"Nothing. A skin problem," he said. "Let's just say she's a little different from most of us, but not too different. I just want you to take her to Otherside where she can catch a freighter to the Mars Colony. Look, I'll pay you two thousand credits to get her to the freight dock safely."

"Okay," I agreed instantly. Two thousand credits was more than I saw in a year, even with a little guns and liquor on the side. "Gimme your ID and I'll check you out," I said. Even for two thousand credits, I couldn't take stupid chances.

He took a plastic card out of a case and slid it over to me. I glanced at it. In big embossed letters it said, "Dayton, Buster Pagliacci." The middle name at least should have impressed me, but it didn't. Once again, I marveled at how parents can make their childrens' lives a living hell by saddling them with stupid names.

I punched him up on my wrist computer. Buster Pagliacci Dayton was a real person. His residence of record was on Earth, in Los Angeles. He was licensed to drive a land vehicle, a light fixed-wing aircraft, and a boat. His location was listed as his Earth residence, so no one knew he was in Mare Tranq. He was forty-seven years old, looked like his identipic, and had only one outstanding felony warrant. For kidnapping.

I punched up the details on the warrant and found that my erstwhile business partner had kidnapped a girl from the Corporation-run National Health Institute's Palos Verdes Facility. No further information was given about the girl, odd in a kidnapping. I mean there should have been a description or a picture or something, just in case someone saw her. Or a name, maybe, at the very least. Weird.

Okay, Buster Pagliacci wanted me to take his kidnap victim to the Mars freighter dock without anyone, like the cops maybe, finding out. It sounded like something I didn't want to get mixed up in.

"Hey, Lizard Breath!" I heard the friendly voice of my sometimes-co-pilot, N'Doro. He must have been drunk, or he would have called me Captain. He pulled up a chair and eyed Buster. "Who's the big guy?"

N'Doro used to be one of the Corporation's rising stars, an Academy graduate with all the right genetic bells and whistles. Then one day he discovered he couldn't take orders any more from a bunch of balding, paunchy old men whose main task in life seemed to be giving him senseless missions. He walked out and came looking for a job in the underbelly of the transportation world. And no one would hire him because no one trusted anyone who came from the Corporation. But I took a chance, even if he was a mite dim sometimes, because he was a fine pilot and extremely good looking in an exotic way.

He rode shotgun on nearly all of my flights except the ones where I didn't want to share the loot.

"Take a look at this," I said, motioning toward Buster Pagliacci Dayton's files. Buster sat in silence.

N'Doro peered at the computer. "Yeah," he said, "I heard about this. Some guy snatched a girl from the Corporation's NHI research facility. There's talk on the street that she might have been carrying some kind of a plague or something. You know, a walking bio-weapon. They're lookin' all over Earth for that guy, only if she was carrying anything really dangerous, he's probably history."

I put the ID card in my purse. "Meet Mr. Dayton, N'Doro. He's not on Earth and he's not history, he's our new client. And I think she's our new cargo. Ready for another run?"

"Are you nuts, Captain?" he asked, suddenly sober. "No amount of money would be enough to transport this kind of cargo! What if it kills us?"

"Two thousand credits. Usual split, sixty-forty?" Eight hundred was more than N'Doro had seen in his entire career, short though it may have been. He thought for a moment.

"Okay," he agreed amiably, "but we gotta check out the kid. I don't wanna mess with anything like viruses or bacterial infections." N'Doro grinned, showing a set of very even, very white teeth against very black and perfect skin. Did I mention that he was built like a brick space station?

Mr. Dayton smiled back, then flagged down a waiter and ordered a bowl of hot steaming goat custards or something, I don't know what.

N'Doro moved close to Mr. Dayton, too close for politeness even in Mare Tranq. I knew he wanted reassurance about the kid.

The goat custards arrived and Dayton sniffed at them, then pushed them away and folded his hands on the table like an expectant child, smiling.

I sighed. "Okay, first off, Mr. Dayton, how'd you find me?"

His smile turned into a grin. He looked at N'Doro and said, "You both were very highly recommended. I spoke to a friend of yours who said you two were the best. He said you guys could fly anything that moved and you were always looking for a little extra work. He also said you were discreet and of high moral principles."

N'Doro frowned. He doesn't like it when people make fun of him. "Who?" He asked tersely.

Dayton looked back at me. "Why, your friend, Mr. Snipely. Lester Snipely."

N'Doro rolled his eyes. Lester Snipely was an ex-pirate we had captured some time ago, back when N'Doro and I worked for The Corporation, in our fatter days. After we had let him go, Snipely married the cargo we were carrying on that trip, namely a Mare Tranq-bound madam named Big Red. We kept his hot little cruiser in case we wanted to do a little pirating on the side for ourselves, but after The Corporation canned us, we had to sell it. It's a long story, not a good one.

"How is old Spray Gun?" I asked. That was Lester's old pirate moniker, Lester Snipely being a bit wuss for a pirate.

"Oh, he's doing fine," Buster Dayton replied. "The business is booming and the missus credits you with turning their lives around. You were pretty easy to find once I knew what to look for-- and where."

"Okay, how'd you meet Lester?" N'Doro's voice was soft, but had an edge to it. Most people answered his questions on the first try, not realizing how dim he really was.

Buster gave N'Doro a thin smile. "I used to date his sister. We kept in touch." It would be easy to give the Snipelys a call and find out.

"Okay," I cut in. "Your ID checks out, but there seems to be a little problem with your, ah, rap sheet. According to the Corporation authorities, you kidnapped a girl from the National Health Institute in Palos Verdes. So how'd you get her here? Who is she? And what's so wrong with her that they won't even publish her identity on the net?"

Buster Pagliacci Dayton didn't say anything for a few minutes. N'Doro leaned back in his chair and cracked his knuckles, an infuriating habit I had tried to break him of on short flights. Buster silently weighed the alternatives and sighed.

N'Doro sat up. I signaled the waiter who brought us a pot of tea, maybe even the real thing this time, and motioned for Buster to get comfy and spill the beans.

"I grew up outside of Los Angeles," he said and N'Doro shifted uneasily. He didn't like those James Michener-type tales that started with the formation of continents on the earth. Cut-To-The-Chase would have been his middle name if he'd more than one to start with.

Buster got the picture and shortened it up. "Anyway, my sister and I had the usual Earthside childhood, then went to local colleges. I went into ergonomic design, and Lag studied marine biology."

"Lag?" I asked.

"Marine biology?" N'Doro asked.

"Lag is short for Lagrima Christi, you know, Tears of Christ." He said this as if I really should have known it, as if it were really a name. Wasn't "Buster Pagliacci" enough? They had to load the daughter up with weird name baggage too? And wouldn't "Christi" have been the logical diminutive? Some people should need a license to breed.

I shot N'Doro an exasperated look. He knew marine biology meant fish, not guys in uniform.

Buster ignored him. "Anyway, I went to work for a design firm in Los Angeles and Lag got a job with the Corporation and the next thing I know Mom's calling me up and telling me there's been a terrible accident and Lag is dead."

I let my tea get cold. Buster had my attention.

"But a body never showed up. I mean none. And the announcement letter was a little odd, too. The Corporation expressed their regret that Lag had suffered a 'terrible accident,' but they didn't say what it was, and no one would give us any information. The whole thing was screwy." Buster shifted in his chair. The one-sixth gravity must have been a blessing to someone of his size.

"Anyway, I knew it couldn't be true. Lag was just too careful for any accident. I figured they must have done something to her. So I did a little snooping around."

I could picture Buster snooping around a high-security place like NHI. They must have bounced his fat ass out of there quicker than you could say Top Secret Government Research.

"I bid for a contract there and got in through my business," he said modestly. "They needed an ergonomic overhaul in the offices. Lots of secretaries had been out with minor work-related injuries and they needed someone to redesign the administration areas. I bid way low just to get in there."

I stared at Buster with admiration. That was a neat trick.

"Anyway, I found out where Lag had been working, but her personnel files were gone. I poked around and found out about a lot of stuff they might have wanted to keep quiet, like how many of their people have died or disappeared or whatever recently."

"So how many?" I asked.

"Twelve in the last two months," he replied.

This was not a significant dip in the overcrowding on Planet Earth, I admit. It would take a cataclysm to even get the numbers down to something conceptually manageable. But for a Corporation research facility, it was pretty high, say in the panic zone.

"And they all worked on the same program as my sister," Buster said.

"So, how'd you decide she wasn't dead after all?" I asked. I was intrigued. Dead was easier, dead was more final. Missing was messy and meant that they needed to keep her alive for something, maybe something really creepy.

"I dunno," Buster confessed. "It was just a feeling. Anyway," he continued, "I scoped out the floor plans of the place and figured she must be in the special ocean project wing somewhere, since that was where she worked. From there it was easy. I had the run of the place during the day, installing furniture and measuring and everything, and I just narrowed it down to a couple of areas. Then I broke in and grabbed her."

He made it sound easy, but the sweat was shining on his face, and Wu's wasn't particularly warm.

"What about the others?" I asked. "The other people who had disappeared on the project."

His face flushed then went pale and sweat ran down one side like a tear. "I-I couldn't, they were, uh, uh. . ." he stuttered." They were too far gone. I couldn't take the chance. I had to leave them."

"What was the matter with them?" I asked. "You know, I'm not going to transport anyone with a plague or anything," I stated flatly, in case I had not made that absolutely clear.

"No, no it's not a plague," he said quickly, "it's nothing like that. It's more like, well, adaptations, sort of. I guess I better let Lag tell you about it."

N'Doro was frowning. "No plague?" He asked. He was fearless except when it came to viruses. They scared the shit out of him, just like everyone else. He looked like he might back out of the deal.

Buster shook his head. "Nothing like that," he repeated. "No danger to us at all, in fact." He sat smiling, hands still folded atop the table.

"Okay, Buster, you're on," I said making the kind of snap decision that gets whole civilizations wiped out. Buster grinned and wanted to shake hands, something I hadn't seen in years. We don't shake hands in space-- it's unsanitary. "Half up front," I said, "and half on delivery. And if you lied and she's infectious, you don't live long enough to pay the second half. Fair enough?"

He nodded, and took out a wallet stuffed with Corporation notes. He counted out a thousand.

"Meet us at the shuttle dock, down at the far end where the contract ships are, tomorrow morning at two. And try to look normal, I got sixteen miners going back to Otherside from a weekend in town here."

Buster picked up the check and N'Doro and I went back to my overnighter.

"I've got a bad feeling about this, Captain," N'Doro said as I counted out his share of the advance money. "He ain't told us everything."

"We don't want to know everything, remember? We already know way too much to lie under the needle." I always preferred plausible deniability, especially where the chemical truth-getter drugs were concerned, but that was unfortunately impossible now.

We slept in my overnighter for a couple of hours, then I packed my few belongings and we checked out. N'Doro and I walked in silence through the dark alleyways to the shuttle dock. The big commercial shuttles were brightly lit, with gleaming paint jobs and crews of busy workers all over them. Next to them were the transport shuttles, big cargo runners that didn't carry passengers, not as fancy, but still impressive. Then there were the private shuttles, small, sleek, and expensive. Finally, there were the contract shuttles like ours, old, peeling, rusting, held together with whatever was handy and would work. The *Linda Rae* looked like she should have been scrapped for parts back when the parts were still worth something.

N'Doro did the safety checks and the mech checks while I straightened up the interior a bit. We could carry twenty passengers, plus ourselves, but the accommodations were anything but plush. The steel seats were welded to the deck and the restraints were wide straps that had frayed in a few places. My expired operator's license hung over the hatch to the bridge cabin.

I slid into the captain's chair and fiddled with the controls. Maybe some of the money from this job could pay for a few improvements, I thought. Like working switches.

My miners were scheduled to show up at two-thirty, but I wanted to be sure Buster and his sister were safely on board and bundled up first. At two o'clock, they arrived, the sister wrapped in a long cloak with a high collar and matching hood that hid most of her face. She was diminutive, at least a foot shorter than Buster, and didn't say a word. Buster ushered her on board and they made themselves as comfortable as possible in the back.

"Hey, Buster, are you going with us?" I was a little surprised. I thought he was going to deliver the cargo and take off. "'Cause if so, the price just went up. You're a wanted fugitive," I reminded him.

"I'm going with her," he said stubbornly. "I'll pay you an extra thousand."

"Okay," I agreed. N'Doro didn't have to know about the extra money. No sense in stretching his mathematical abilities.

The miners, a grey-faced lot who worked the Corporation mines north of Otherside, boarded quietly. They were all well and truly hung-over and I knew they wouldn't be doing any unnecessary talking for the trip, and maybe not even any unnecessary breathing.

N'Doro fastened the locks from the inside and I ran the pressurization. Then I flipped the switches back and forth a couple of times as they weren't too reliable, and the big engines started up as N'Doro slipped into the co-pilot's seat beside me. Control cleared us for takeoff and we were almost out of the gate when the panicky voice of Control broke into my pre-flight reverie demanding that we return.

"Sorry," I shouted into the radio, "I can't hear you!" There was a lot of static from dirty switches and ancient equipment. But I didn't need to listen to them to know what it was all about. We cleared the dome that enclosed Mare Tranq and I glanced back at Lag or whatever her name was. She hadn't moved a muscle.

The trip to Otherside was the usual, except that N'Doro kept looking back at the passengers, something he never did when it was just a bunch of miners.

"Relax," I said to him. "I've got a plan." I said this with a great deal of self-confidence and very little truth.

"As soon as we get there," I said, making it up as I went along, "I'll grab Buster and the girl and we'll make a run for it while you offload the miners, maybe get into a fight with a couple of them. By the time the Port Police sort it all out, we'll be long gone, and you'll just have an assault complaint or something." Sounded good to me.

N'Doro wasn't convinced, but it was the closest thing we had to a real plan. And anyway, it was what always worked for us when we had other kinds of volatile cargo. Like the time we... well, never mind.

So as soon as we got down and under the dome at Otherside, but before the Corporation cops or the Port Police could get out to our end of the dock, me, Buster and the girl were gone. N'Doro's white teeth were flashing as he soundly annoyed a dozen hung-over miners.

Buster practically carried his little sister and I led the way, twisting through a bunch of rust-covered derelict shuttles and miscellaneous debris. Otherside is not a very pretty place.

I ducked down a hole and into what looked like a large sewer. The door at the end of the tunnel swung open and we were whisked inside.

It was bright, smoky, smelly, loud and felt safe. Annie's Underground was the usual hangout for shuttle rats, and she could tell I needed a back door quick. We ran through to the other side of the bar where another tunnel led out to a solid wall of moonrock. As the door clanged shut behind us, plunging us into absolute darkness, I heard Buster gasp. "I don't like the dark," he said in the precursor of a whine.

"Oh, shut up," I said, pressing an outcropping of rock above my head and twisting it. Another tunnel opened ahead of us, this one with low wattage emergency lighting. "We can't stay here," I said. "I still have to get you to the Mars dock. But we can rest for a bit."

Lag took off her coat, lowering the hood which had concealed most of her face. Her skin was a luminescent green and she held a gelpack of thickened water over her nose, breathing from it. A bony ridge of iridescent green scales grew from the back of her neck. Her hands were similarly scale-covered and the fingers were webbed, ending in sharp, curving claws. There were more biogel packs laid over slits along her neck – gills. I guessed I had seen iguanas of a more pleasing countenance.

"What the hell is she?" I asked Buster.

Before he could answer, Lag removed her breathing pack. "It's okay," she said, "I don't look it, but I'm still human. This is what they were doing at the Health Institute. I'm one of the more successful experiments."

If that was success, I didn't want to see the failures.

"Why?" I asked. For someone to go through that kind of trouble, there's gotta be funded research on a very large scale, no pun intended. And there would have to be an objective.

"I was a prototype for the Mars colony," she said. I knew Mars was riddled with great, mostly frozen underground oceans composed primarily of water and dissolved carbon dioxide, with traces of all the usual dirt and minerals thrown in for good measure, winding seas spiraling toward the core of the planet. What a mantle looks like when most of the original planet was an iceball. They had never really been explored, to my knowledge. Our colonies were supposedly all above-ground, like on the moon. "The Corporation wants to expand into the planet, and to do that, they need people who have a good scientific background, but who are adapted to live there. But the adaptation process has had a few glitches."

"You don't say," I agreed.

"The first adapted people were volunteers, of course. I'm afraid you saw some of them," she said to her brother. It was uncanny-- under the scaly surface, there was a definite family resemblance. He nodded and looked as if he might be sick. "They were not successful. So," she continued, "they stopped using volunteers."

I let the full horror sink in. "They did *this* to you without your consent?"

She nodded, a weird motion, what with the neck ridge, gill slits and all. I noticed that the irises of her eyes were an odd shape and two tiny winglike appendages came out of her back. Her nostrils flared and steam issued forth. She clamped the gelpack back in place.

"How?" I asked, fascinated by her appearance.

"Gene splicing techniques," she said. "Pretty simple stuff, really. The remarkable part is what they spliced me with. I'm no ordinary lizard," she said, laughing. "The oceans of Mars have very little life left in them, you know, even though they are the key to rich mineral deposits. The core is cooling down, and the mantle seas are freezing solid, except around Mons Olympus and Tharsis, and some of the other still-active volcanic regions. It won't be long, geologically. But there is a creature who has survived in that environment. It was once a sort of flying amphibian. One of those is my new brother or father or whatever-- a new part of me. I am a new creature, created just for the spiral seas."

I shuddered. I had heard of the Martian dragons, of course. But just as fossils in the surface rocks. Not for a million credits, I thought. "So why'd you let Buster kidnap you?" I asked. "Why not just wait and go there with the Corporation's blessing?"

There was a pause. "I - I don't know how to explain this part," she said. "I need to get there quickly, before the Corporation finishes their experiments. I am not a finished product," she reminded me. "But I am an important one. The others, the ones in the oceans, are able to communicate with me. I have to get to them. We have to do something before the Corporation ruins the underground seas. Don't you see? They know what's coming. They are intelligent."

"Intelligent life on Mars?" I squeaked incredulously. It was a joke that not even the Corporation could qualify in that department.

Lag nodded. "I'm it. Well, part of it. When I join the others, with what I carry, we will become powerful enough to resist them."

It looked pretty hopeless to me. The Corporation was the most powerful thing in the universe, controlling all politics and almost all commerce. Those who survived outside of it, like me, could hardly ever be described as successful. This delicate little dragon girl didn't stand a chance. But I felt myself ready to be convinced.

"Can you really do that?" I asked.

Lag nodded. "I've developed some abilities I never had before. Things the Corporation never suspected the dragons could do. Telepathy, for one thing. But greatly amplified. That's how I was able to get Buster to free me. But I don't want to convince you that way. I want you to know what's happening, what will happen, and see that I have to get there and do this thing."

"Okay," I said, but details bore me. "Whatever. But if we want to make the Mars ship, we'll have to leave now."

Buster helped her on with her coat and hood and we set off through the maze of tunnels at a brisk trot, the tiniest hint of a tail dragging along behind her.

I knew the way. I had smuggled a few people and a couple of other items through the tunnels of Otherside before. I found the hatch that led to the Mars docks and cautioned Buster and his sister to stay very quiet. He pulled her to him and shielded her small form with his bulk.

I poked my head through the hatch and looked around. We were definitely at the Mars dock, and the big freighters made the little lunar shuttles look like toys. There weren't any cops around, and all the activity seemed to center on one big ship that was being readied for the twenty-one day trip to Mars Colony.

"Got your tickets, folks?" I asked as I helped them through the hatch. It was dark out, but the freighter was brightly lit.

"I don't think we'll have too much trouble," Lag said in her soft, hissing voice. "Many of those workers have been to Mars," she said, "and they will listen to me with their minds more readily than those who have not."

She hugged Buster. "You know what to do," she said to him and he nodded. She turned to me. "Thank you for all you have done. In the future, when we sing in the great spiraling oceans of our victories over the intruders, your part will not be forgotten and you will live forever in our history."

"Forever? But your seas are freezing, Lag."

"We shall not let them," she said simply.

I looked into her eyes, into those oddly shaped irises, and felt a surge of warmth flow over me. Then she was gone, a tiny, lonely figure walking toward the hull of the great freighter.

We waited until she was aboard, then I led Buster back through the tunnels to Annie's. I ordered us each a drink as he counted out the rest of my money.

"So, what are your plans?" I asked. "If you need a ride back to Mare Tranq, we can probably swing something." But he didn't need a ride back. He told me his plans and I broke out in a cold sweat, even though Annie kept the thermostat in her place at around boiling.

"What do you mean?" I asked, terrified of his answer.

He showed me his hands. They were already starting to scale over a bit, and the greenish tinge to his face wasn't from the heat or Annie's drinks. My stomach turned.

"It- it *is* a virus, isn't it?" I asked in a petrified whisper.

He nodded. "But don't worry," he said. "You're perfectly safe. I- I injected myself with it at the NHI. You can't catch it through casual contact."

Yeah, I thought. That's what they said about Andele Seven, but it took two point six three million deaths before the Corporation admitted their mistake on that one.

"Why?" I asked, gulping down the last of my drink and signaling Annie for another. I needed it.

"I want to help," Buster replied. "I want people to know what's going on, what the Corporation is doing on Mars. I want everyone to know there is intelligent life out there, even if it does look a little different. And I want this whole lab in Palos Verdes exposed." He looked so earnest, so hopeful.

I left him there at Annie's, staring thoughtfully into a drink.

I got back to my shuttle and found the Corporation cops and the Port Police duking it out over jurisdiction. The Port Police won, and I was forced to update my operator's license, get a bunch of stuff on the *Linda Rae* fixed and pay a hefty fine or bribe or whatever to the local magistrate. So much for my windfall from Buster. No hint of suspicion about my previous cargo, though.

I picked N'Doro up at the jail and got another load of miners, this batch on their way to some R & R at Mare Tranq and eager to get a head start. Usually I let them know right away that there's an extra charge for partying, but this time I was too preoccupied to even notice.

On the way to Mare Tranq I told N'Doro what had happened, leaving out the part about Lag having a virus and Buster catching it. For a couple of months, we scanned the news, looking for any mention of the Mars Colony oceans. There wasn't any. And I checked my skin every morning for any telltale green places or scales, but never found anything more than brown spots from solar radiation and the occasional tattoo.

So maybe it was all only a whacked-out story from a couple of weird kids with a skin disease. Or maybe we just haven't heard from the dragons in the Martian spiral seas.

One of the Family

Sometimes there's a little family story to tell – Cookie Sullivan, Captain of the Linda Rae, found this in with a batch of her father's letters after his death. She's still looking for her half-sister, Elaine – and Roger, of course

I eased the throttle back slowly and the glider came to a smooth halt in front of Myron's Pet Shop. I jumped out, still proud of the way I looked in my tight-fitting uniform. When I removed my helmet and shook out my hair, I knew I could pass for twenty-five at a distance. I smiled.

I wasn't there to give Myron any trouble - not that he didn't deserve it, the slimeball. I was there to see if the shipment of kitties had arrived yet. I wanted to get a nice little kitty to replace dear departed old Spot, my previous pet. I was wearing my Immigration Service uniform, but I wasn't on business.

I know, I know, I get a lot of rhetoric from the locals who think we should just drop our immigration restrictions and let every off-worlder in the whole damned universe move in and take advantage of our free air and water. But you tell that to the patient taxpayers who can't even afford a sightseeing trip to Mare Tranq, much less ... well, I'm sure you've heard all the arguments before, too.

Anyway, I was just there to check on the kitties. I went into the shop and was immediately assailed by the smell. It was a fecund mixture of rotting sawdust, stale lettuce, moldy pet foods and unclean cages filled with the excrement of a dozen species, including some very large reptiles. "Myron!" I called. "It's Elaine, got the kitties in yet?" Part of the smell was Myron, too. The worst part.

"Ovah heah, Sugarpants," Myron's heavily accented and wheezing voice came from a dim corner where the lights of fish tanks glowed in different colors.

Myron was short, about five-five tops, but what he lacked in height he made up for in girth. He was as wide as the aisles, which I knew for a fact had been widened recently just to accommodate him, never mind the customers. He was sweating and the scent that wafted from him made the neglected cages smell wholesome. He was also one of those specimens of humanity that made you question the definition of the term.

Our immigration restrictions seemed weird to some folks. I mean, if you were a family from the New Mars Colony and you still looked sort of human, you could move back to good ole Earth anytime. But if you were say, a family from

Mare Tranquillitatis, the first moon base, and you hadn't lived on Earth for several generations, then things were a little different. And if you were a true off-worlder who had never been human, then you had to go through a laborious process to make Earth your new home. These cases were all pretty easy to figure out.

It was the In Betweens who made life difficult.

IB's were those folks who had one human parent or grandparent or who looked sorta human, but had something different about them, like Myron's girlfriend, the one who almost got sold by mistake in the shop one day when she was taking a nap in one of the heated reptile pens. Her scaly skin ... well, it was just a mistake.

Ever since we had simultaneously colonized our own moon and made contact with two other sentient species who came to congratulate us on this momentous feat, we'd had trouble with our immigration. At first, there were just prudent quarantine policies designed to filter out new and lethal viruses and diseases. But the Rigelians, who could interbreed, swarmed to Earth by the millions in the first few months. Fortunately, they were pretty easy to spot, what with their short stature and glowing blue skin.

Myron was an IB, the usual offspring of an Earth mother and Rigelian father, sort of. The Rigelians could mate with either sex of nearly all the mammals found on Earth, but seemed to prefer human women. Myron was at least half-human and born on Earth and could prove it, so he got to stay and I never hassled him over that.

But I did hassle him over his relatives and his countless siblings and the visas he reputedly sold over the counter in his shop. The kitties I was waiting for probably had some Rigelian in them. This was disturbing, but it was hard to find a domestic animal that didn't have some Rigelian in it somewhere. A hundred years of indiscriminate mating on the part of the Rigelians, not to mention the humans, too, had left the gene pool pretty muddy.

The Mating Restriction Act went into effect long after the damage had been done.

Once in a while Myron's mother, who was still around and still had a fondness for Rigelians, would try to pass off some cousin or something as half-human just to get a permanent residence visa. There was a thriving black market for these visas, especially in sales to the other side, namely the Chorons.

The Chorons were the other species that made contact. While the Rigelians were squat, smelly and somewhat humanoid, willing and able to mate with anything that would stand still long enough for it, the Chorons were completely different. They were planal, like glass, and cerebral, controlling their external world through a complicated series of electrical commands that translated into a kinetic energy. They communicated with humans by means of electrical impulses directed to the brain. It was efficient and effective and felt like a snowstorm inside your head when they were doing it. They had no interest in sex whatsoever and seemed to have no need for reproduction, as their population did not appear to fluctuate.

But they liked life on Earth -- they seemed to have an immense capacity for sensory appreciation when it came to beautiful views, fine music and the like. They were just too different from us to communicate in any way that would make us like them.

Of the two, I am embarrassed to say that humanity seemed to prefer the randy Rigelians. So much for lofty intellectual pursuit.

Nearly fifteen years in the Immigration Service had shown me a few things you wouldn't want to know about, and taught me a few lessons no one should have to learn the hard way, but it had also been a good way to learn about the off-worlders. And it instilled an appreciation for the planet that could border on fanaticism if I let it.

"I'm looking for the kitties," I said to Myron. He had a hand in a fish tank, feeding something to a glowing blue fish. There was something oddly familiar about the color.

He saw my expression and laughed. "Don't even think it, Sweetpea," he said. "This is a fish. We don't do fish. It comes by this color nachurly." He finished feeding the fish and dried his hands on a towel. "They right back heah," he said, motioning to the delivery room.

The delivery room was a large bay, with exposed rafters and unfinished walls. The floor was poured concrete and cold under my boots. There was a large crate in the middle of the floor with air holes in it. I saw a little paw wave through a hole and then a tiny pink nose try to push out.

The kitties!

They were so cute I almost forgave Myron for being such a sack of rotted mulch. There were about eight of them, all mewling and squirming and trying out their tiny claws. I looked for an orange-and-white one, but those big ginger-tom types had sort of disappeared in the last decade or so, replaced by big blue-and-white ones. There was a small all-blue one with a pink face and white little paws. It looked up at me and I knew it was the one.

I picked him up and he was wonderful, purring like a glider engine in my ear, little needle claws digging into my uniform.

"Okay, Myron," I said, "I'll take this little guy." I was thinking of a name for him. I didn't have anything picked out.

Myron looked uncomfortable. "Whyn't 'chall take this one?" he said, holding up a little bundle of white fur. It was cute, too, the smiling little furball. But I had made my choice.

"Nope," I said. "This is the one. How much I owe ya?"

Myron was sweating, not that he didn't always sweat. He moved from one foot to the other and refused to meet my eyes. "Please pick another one," he begged.

"Why? This is the one I want." I stared at him with irritation, my good mood rapidly evaporating. "Is there something wrong with this one, Myron? Is there something wrong with this whole shipment of kitties?" I had one hand on my pistol belt.

"N-no, go ahead, take whatchu wan'." He backed away from me.

I went back out into the main pet shop and swiped my card through the reader, authorizing the cost of the cat. Then I put the little baby in my luggage compartment, put on my helmet, and gunned the glider.

Over the course of the next few weeks I broke up a Choron visa ring, busted a Rigelian smuggler, put through visa applications for 16 miners from the Mars Colony who had been born there but didn't like the work, and fed the growing kitten. The kitten grew like nothing you have ever seen.

I named him "Roger," after an old friend. Roger weighed 14 pounds when I took him to the vet for his shots.

"You can't be serious," the vet said when I mentioned that Roger was only a couple of months old. "This cat looks full-grown, maybe a year or a year and a half."

"No, he was only a tiny baby a few weeks ago," I explained. "I think he just grew fast." The explanation sounded a little lame to me, too. But it was true. Roger had grown tremendously in a short time.

Roger was the most affectionate kitty I ever saw. He was smart, too, and he grew more beautiful every day. And bigger. He was just like one of the family.

In less than two months after I got him, Roger was the size of a small mountain lion and still growing. I stopped feeding him canned cat food and started buying farmed meat from the local market. He liked it and continued to grow.

I knew there was something different about Roger, but I had grown to love him. I didn't want to lose him. Every evening when I got home, he would comb my hair with his claws, then he would knead the muscles in my back with his big, gentle paws. After I was relaxed, I would brush his fur until he purred himself to sleep. Then I would fix us both dinner, something frozen for me and farmed meat for him, and we would watch the video for a while. Sometimes I just fell asleep against his big warm body, his clean-smelling fur next to my face. Roger was all I wanted.

In the mornings, we played with an old pillow. I threw it across the room and Roger pounced, dragging it back and teasing me with it until I grabbed it and threw it again. Sometimes we wrestled a bit, but Roger always kept his claws in so as not to injure me. He was very strong by then, but all I had to do was cry out and he would let me go.

When he was the size of a tiger, I knew I would have to do something. Feeding him was expensive but not difficult, and his little litter box had become a regular waste-disposal system just like anything you or I would use. But I was too nervous to take him to the vet's again, even though I wanted to be sure he was in the best of health. I was afraid someone would see him.

I went back to Myron's.

"Ah bin espectin' y'all," he drawled. He finished feeding a head of romaine to a pair of hungry iguanas. "How's your kitty doin'?"

"That's what I wanted to discuss with you, Myron," I said. I shut the front door of the shop and turned the "Open" sign around so no one would bother us.

"They weren't regular kitties, were they?" I asked.

Myron kept his head down, watching the prehistoric creatures munch the greenery. He didn't answer.

"Myron, do you have any idea how big Roger is?" I asked. "He's the size of a tiger, for Chrissakes! What's wrong with him?"

"Ain't nuthin' wrong," he drawled. "Jes' got chu a big kitty is all. He a nice kitty?"

"Yeah, he's wonderful," I said, "he's the best kitty I've ever seen in my life, Myron, but he's not a normal kitty! He's bigger than I am!"

"Do he talk to you, Sweetpea?" Myron asked.

"Whaddaya mean, talk to me? No, he doesn't talk to me. He's a cat, Myron!"

"You sure, Sugar?"

Well, I was pretty sure that Roger didn't talk to me, but I wasn't sure he was a cat. I mean, I wasn't sure he was *just* a cat. "Myron, is there something here I should know about? Because if you don't loosen up right this minute, I'm going to poke your fat ass with a great big pin and listen to all the hot air come screaming out." I unhooked my baton from my pistol belt and pulled the endcap off it. A six-inch steel spike gleamed in the fetid air.

Myron backed up against a glass case full of tiny chirping birds. "Ah tried to git chu t' take anuthuh one," he whined. "Ah din't wan' chu takin' thet one!"

"Why, Myron? What was wrong with him?"

"Aw, shoot, Elaine!" he whined. "If ah tell you whut, you jus' gonna git mad and thet pore kitty ain't gonna have no home!" Myron's blue-tinged skin glistened with sweat.

I couldn't imagine Roger homeless. He would always have a home with me, no matter what. I loved that cat more than anything, more than any human, half-human, alien, or what have you I had ever met. I understood all those elderly women who gave up the company of ornery and smelly old men for the company of sleek and beautiful cats.

"Don't be stupid, Myron!" I said. "Roger will always live with me. I love that cat. Now what's wrong with him?"

Myron told me.

"You're a liar!" I screamed. I ran out of there and vomited before I reached the curb, splattering my shiny jackboots with my lunch.

It's been three months since I saw Myron. Roger continued to grow a bit more, but seems to have stabilized at about the size of a lion. I keep him indoors all of the time now, but he doesn't seem to mind. He runs on my treadmill for exercise and climbs up and down the stairs. He eats well and still likes to play with the pillow. He's as affectionate as ever and still combs my hair and kneads my back for me. He doesn't talk, though.

But Myron was right. I guess I should get rid of Roger, but it's too hard to think about it. You see, Roger is nearly full-grown now, and will want a mate soon. And as much as I adore Roger, the thought of mating with Myron's brother turns my stomach.

ACKNOWLEDGEMENTS

Many of these stories were previously published and I would like to thank the editors of those magazines for their generous support. They made the Universe a more interesting place, and made me long to be a part of that alternate future we all want to explore.

A big thank you to **Dan Hollifield**, editor of **Aphelion: The Webzine of Science Fiction and Fantasy**, where many of these stories first saw print. *CAPTAIN'S LOG, LANGUAGE BARRIER, CAUSE AND EFFECT, THERE IS ALWAYS A REASON, ROOTS, THE TANNEH DEATH CHOP – DAN'S STORY, VINNIE'S CARGO,* and *CHUMP CHANGE* were all featured in Aphelion. A special thank you to Dan for his wonderful creation of the Mare Inebrium and his permission to use it here, and for publishing so many of my stories.

Aphelion Webzine may be accessed here: **http://www.aphelion-webzine.com/**   Go on, try it – it's free.

Thank you to **Jack Egan**, whose beautiful magazine, **The Spiral Sea**, featured *THE SPIRAL SEAS* with Jack's original color illustration in its inaugural issue. You can find it on the web here: **http://www.spiralsea.com/aug2001/spiralsea_fiction_spiralseas_thornton.html**

And finally, thank you to **Andrew G. McCann**, whose **Planet Magazine** has been online and in full color since 1994, for publishing *ONE OF THE FAMILY*, with a beautiful illustration by artist Romeo Esparrago. It is certainly worth a look:

http://planetmagazine.com/pm18/family.htm

BACK TO TANNEH was written especially for this collection. I just had to find out what happened…

KATE THORNTON has been writing mystery and science fiction for several decades. A retired US Army officer, she is a member of the Los Angeles Chapter of Sisters in Crime and is a regular contributor to their anthologies. She teaches a short story class whenever the mood strikes. You may contact her at her website:

http://www.katethornton.net/

Made in the USA
Las Vegas, NV
09 January 2022

40981895R00146